I caught my b... walked to the gr... of the old theater. I walked past the hollow eyes of cobwebbed ticket booths into a decrepit yet ornate foyer; huge crystal chandeliers, their bulbs dimly flickering, guided my way.

I called out, "Hello! Danny?"

I started up a curved, worn-carpeted staircase. Then I caught my own reflection in a large, cracked wall mirror, but I saw something else as well, something, *someone*, stumbling up behind me.

Where he came from, I'm not sure. But when I whirled, Danny Brown was suddenly standing in front of me and between his eyes was a small, dark, irregular circle that I knew, somehow, though I'd never before seen one, was a bullet hole. . . .

I LOVE TROUBLE

I
LOVE
TROUBLE

———

A novel by Peter Brackett

based on a screenplay
by Nancy Myers and
Charles Shyer

Ⓢ
A SIGNET BOOK

SIGNET
Published by the Penguin Group
Penguin Books USA Inc., 375 Hudson Street,
New York, New York 10014, U.S.A.
Penguin Books Ltd, 27 Wrights Lane,
London W8 5TZ, England
Penguin Books Australia Ltd, Ringwood,
Victoria, Australia
Penguin Books Canada Ltd, 10 Alcorn Avenue,
Toronto, Ontario, Canada M4V 3B2
Penguin Books (N.Z.) Ltd, 182-190 Wairau Road,
Auckland 10, New Zealand

Penguin Books Ltd, Registered Offices:
Harmondsworth, Middlesex, England

First published by Signet, an imprint of Dutton Signet,
a division of Penguin Books USA Inc.

First Printing, July, 1994
10 9 8 7 6 5 4 3 2 1

 REGISTERED TRADEMARK—MARCA REGISTRADA

Printed in the United States of America

PUBLISHER'S NOTE
This is a work of fiction. Names, characters, places, and incidents either are the
product of the author's imagination or are used fictitiously, and any resemblance to
actual persons, living or dead, events, or locales is entirely coincidental.

To Max Allan Collins . . .
without whom this book
couldn't have been written

1

An Innocent
Beginning

—

BYLINE: Peter Brackett

It started innocently enough.

Imagine a serenely bucolic landscape, like one of those cornball prints that were fashionable around the turn of the century: cows grazing lazily in a green pasture, wildflowers bending gently in the morning breeze. The last setting in the world where you'd expect to find guns and murder and greed.

Or romance, for that matter.

But it did begin there, all right, although before long things took a predictable turn for the even worse in (naturally) the big city, albeit a big city built in the midst of American's heartland on what once was a marsh (you wouldn't want to waste good farmland building a city, would you?), a city of "big shoulders" (as Carl Sandburg once put it) where the skyscraper was born, a city once known as the Cattle Butcher to America, a city where half a dozen major newspapers once thrived and now only two remain.

I wasn't there when any of it started—not at the hillside funeral in Wisconsin, not in State Street Station when an assassin followed his victim onto a train filled with innocent bystanders who would also become victims. No, I wasn't there. But then reporters almost never are in at the start of story.

What's important is to be there at the finish.

Now, I know it's fashionable in these days of "investigative reporting" to have an image of Woodward and Bernstein behaving like hybrids of Mike Hammer and James Bond in not only rooting out the truth, but literally *making* news. Becoming the story yourself.

Generally, I don't approve of that. A good reporter reports on the news, and, on the Op Ed page, comments on it. You don't *make* news.

Sometimes, however, it can't be helped, and in this case I wound up helping make a certain amount of news myself, which requires some explanation, which is why I ended up collaborating on this book with Sabrina Peterson, who works for the *other* paper in Chicago.

Collaborations are always a compromise, and what we've decided to do (since I witnessed certain events that Ms. Peterson did not, and vice versa) is trade off chapters. Because, typically, I had the jump on her, where the story is concerned, the first several chapters will be mine. Once Sabrina has made her entrance, we'll alternate. Clear?

Oh, and before we press on, an important point: opinions expressed herein by Ms. Peterson do not necessarily (in fact, usually don't) mirror those of my own.

But our decision to jointly sell to Hollywood the rights of our respective coverage of what has come to be known as "The LDF Cover-up," for docudrama purposes, has put Ms. Peterson and me in bed together (so to speak).

And before I begin this narrative properly, I want to make a few things "perfectly clear" (as somebody once said).

First of all, the title. *I Love Trouble* was *not* my idea, nor was it Ms. Peterson's, though she may claim otherwise. It was the creation of the Hollywood screenwriters, in an apparent effort to invoke warm-and-fuzzy memories of 1940s screwball comedies. I can assure you that the experiences Ms. Peterson and I managed to live through were hardly comedic, and I can further assure you that I do *not* love trouble.

Nor do I look like Cary Grant or Clark Gable, though at six two and as a well-preserved, (early) forty-something with a minimum of flab and retaining all of my sandy blond hair, I can still get a smile or two out of a pretty salesgirl (a politically incorrect term, but if I note every politically incorrect term I use, we're *never* going to get this thing off the ground). Immodest as it may sound, I'm not the kind of guy who has much trouble getting the best table in a restaurant, or making new friends at a cocktail party.

And Sabrina Peterson does not resemble Claudette Colbert or Katherine Hepburn, either, though truth be told she's easy enough on the eyes. It would probably get her feminist dander up if I mentioned she has a sweet slender shape, and incredible brown eyes, a cascade of reddish-brown hair, and a smile as wide as it is sparkling.

So I won't.

The other thing you may be wondering is why in God's name would Peter Brackett—whose five-days-a-week Chicago column in the *Chronicle* has made him a household name in the Windy City, whose first novel, *White Lies*, was on the *New York Times* hardcover fiction bestseller list two weeks longer than the latest Dean Koontz—would bother contributing to a "quickie" current-event-type paperback.

It's this simple: if I didn't do this myself, some faceless hack would no doubt do so, creating a "movie tie-in" for the docudrama that is being filmed even as I write this.

By writing this book (with Ms. Peterson's help), I give you, the reader, the opportunity to compare what *really* happened to whatever Hollywood chooses to tell you happened. Don't get me wrong: I took the Hollywood money, so my indignation can only go *so* far. But I view this book as an opportunity to set the record straight.

Even if Sabrina Peterson does get the same opportunity.

Where it really began for me was late one Thursday afternoon. The setting sun was shooting blinding brilliant streaks between the skyscrapers, one of which—the gothic limestone *Chronicle* Building on North Michigan Avenue—was home. We pulled up at the curb.

That is, she pulled up at the curb, the lovely blonde whose name escapes me, in a red Miata whose gleaming hood was catching those reflective streaks of sun, and winking at us.

She was giving me a quick good-bye kiss, which consisted of wrapping me up in her clinging arms and endless legs and her pile of sweet-smelling blond hair, and planting on yours truly one of those suck-the-chrome-off-the-fender-of-a-'57-Chevy kisses.

When I finally came up for air, I managed, "Thanks for the lift."

"I don't think I've ever been to a more memorable book signing," she purred. She really did: she purred.

I slipped my tie off her neck and loosely slipped it back around my own open shirt collar.

"This one was right up there for me, too," I admitted, and I kissed her hand (corny, but it works), and headed toward the entry to the *Chronicle* building, slipping on my sports coat, smoothing out my slacks.

"Peter!"

I turned, and she was leaning out the Miata, her lovely frame draped across the passenger seat, holding out of the window a copy of my novel. The hardcover edition.

"You never got around to *signing* it!" she called, laughing a little.

I went over to her, and tried to think of something clever and endearing to write. Any real writer will tell you that writing books is easy—coming up with a personalized inscription to write in a copy of one of your books, other than "best wishes," *that's* the hard part.

I glanced up and a bus was gliding by, bearing my own smiling photo—a decidedly less rumpled, several years younger version of me, I admit (book signing can take it out of a guy)—and the familiar tagline the *Chronicle*'s been using to sell me, the last couple of years: CHICAGO WOULDN'T BE CHICAGO WITHOUT PETER BRACKETT—READ HIM TODAY.

So I signed the book, "Chicago wouldn't be Chicago without . . ." and then I put in *her* name (which, as I said, has since slipped my mind). Anyway, that made her beam and almost blush and then she and her Miata were gone, and I was snugging my tie into place as I entered the *Chronicle*'s cathedrallike lobby.

I took the elevator up to the bustling city room, where across the sprawling sea of desks where minions clicked-clacked at computer terminals, I could see the glassed-in offices belonging to those of us higher up the food chain.

And in my office, toward the rear of the newsroom, I could see an apparent re-creation of the stateroom scene in *A Night at the Opera*: crowded in there were half a dozen people, plus Jeannie, blond, handsomely middle-aged, and businesslike in her gray coatdress, looking more like the boss than a topflight secretary to one of the city's top columnists. Jeannie, her cool efficiency severely taxed, was milling around among them like a frazzled air traffic controller.

Seeing that traffic jam in my office, my first instinct was to go somewhere else. I did an about-face and nearly ran smack into an attractive if vaguely disheveled young woman whose arms were piled with clipping-bulging files.

I startled her, but then she melted.

She was a fan.

"Sorry," I said. "We almost had a disaster, there."

"It was my fault!"

"No it wasn't," I said, faintly amused. I touched

her arm gently and leaned in conspiratorially. "Do me a favor."

Her eyes were blue and bright; they got brighter. "Yes?"

"Walk me outside for a minute."

She seemed stunned that I would actually speak to her. Then she nodded and followed me into the hallway.

"This is an honor," she said.

"Walking me into the hall?"

"I can't believe I'm actually finally meeting you! I've read every column you've ever written."

"I wish I could say as much. At this stage, I've written more than a few in my sleep."

"I can't believe *that*! I've been working here nine months, Mr. Brackett, and this is the first I've even *seen* you."

"I work odd hours. I modem a lot my stuff in from home." I glanced back toward the newsroom, visible through a wall of mostly windows.

"I know you've been busy promoting your novel, which I have to tell you I've already read twice—"

"What are you working on?"

She glanced at her armload of clips. "Obituaries."

"You've been here nine months and they still have you researching obits?"

She nodded numbly. "Is that wrong?"

"You tell Greenfield if you'd wanted to do research, you'd've become a librarian. Tell him you came here to be a reporter, and that you're willing to report on anything, any time, any day."

"You think I'd really get anywhere? Wouldn't that be . . . kind of presumptuous on my part?"

"Not when you've had a better offer from the *Globe*."

"But . . . I haven't had a better offer from the *Globe*."

"Does he know that?"

She smiled, cocked her head. "You really think that would work?"

"Did for me. What's your name?"

"Evans." She managed to extend hand around the armful of files. "Cindy Evans."

I shook her hand. "Pleased to meet you, Evans. You got a quarter?"

She juggled the files, slipping a hand into her jacket pocket, and withdrew a palmful of change. "Help yourself."

I plucked out a quarter and thanked her. "Pay you back," I said, heading for a phone booth.

"You already have!" she called behind me.

The phone booths at the *Chronicle* have been here almost as long as the building itself; they're the old-fashioned kind that you can close yourself into. The gradual disappearance of these wood-and-glass wombs is one of the great cultural losses of the late twentieth century.

I dropped the quarter in the slot and dialed my own number. Soon Jeannie's voice was saying, "Peter Brackett's office."

She was having to raise her voice over the noise of the crowd.

"Who are those people *in* Peter Brackett's office?" I asked. I didn't have to identify myself: She knew the voice.

"Your publicist," she whispered. "Also, a guy with a bone to pick from Alderman Cvack's office . . ."

"Oh, hell."

". . . Sully, who says he's got the informant's tape . . ."

"Great!"

". . . but has to give it to you 'personal.' "

"Shit."

"And a messenger from Marshall Field's with a pair of three-hundred-dollar loafers that only *you* can sign for, as well as a photographer who's supposed to shoot your new eight by ten's. There's a couple more. By the way, you do realize your column is due in nine minutes?"

"Sarcasm is unbecoming of a woman of your dignity, Jeannie."

"Nine minutes," she said, savoring it. "This could be a record—even for you."

"You call Guinness. I got a column to write. In the meantime, tell everyone I called in sick. It's that Asian kinda flu that lasts two months."

"Understood."

"Sign for the shoes, pay Sully for the tape—"

"Peter," a voice from the phone said.

Not Jeannie's. This was a voice as soothing as fingernails caressing a chalkboard.

"Hi, Lindy," I said. Lindy was my publicist. She treated me like a disobedient child. I've had considerable practice being treated that way.

"Honey, listen. I can *not* set up these prestigious book signings if you're gonna make a cameo appearance in the story of your own life."

"Hey, I signed a lot of books—"

"You were there five minutes, and then disappeared with that blonde with the legs that went *all* the way up."

"She was just giving me a lift home. Lindy, give

me a little credit, will ya? Who was the caterer on those hors d'oeuvres, anyway? The Tylenol killer?"

"You got sick, sweetie?"

"Sicker than Rush Limbaugh's politics, dollface," I said. I weakened my voice. "I'm in bed at this very moment. Food poisoning. I can barely form the words."

A tap on the window of the phone booth caught my attention, and I turned to see the well-worn, world-weary puss of my managing editor, Matt Greenfield, glowering at me. Matt's in his late fifties and looks every year of it, his bifocals on a cord around his neck like a badge of middle age. He pointed to his watch and lifted one eyebrow, Mr. Spock-style.

I opened the door a crack. "The damn thing's written!"

"Really?"

"I swear. I just need to proof it. You'll have the column in three minutes."

That would be a record even Jeannie would be impressed by.

Just behind Matt, the newsroom door opened and Matt turned to look as a noisy parade of my would-be visitors began tromping out with the scowling complainer from Alderman Cvack's office in the lead. I ducked down, opened the door and, keeping low like any smart soldier behind enemy lines, went in the opposite direction, leaving them all behind.

Including my managing editor, who had long since gotten used to my ability to disappear at will.

2

A Well-Turned Calf

BYLINE: Peter Brackett

Despite the wall of glass next to me, beyond which the *Chronicle* city room was gradually thinning out, I was in a sort of sanctuary in my inner office. My secretary knew not to disturb me. No one could enter while I was making magic.

The trick I was performing at the moment was, admittedly, a somewhat underhanded one, albeit not uncommon in the columnist trade. I had glimpsed a story in today's *Chronicle* about a shooting at Woodfield Mall involving a teenage boy, which reminded me of a similar tragedy, years before. On my computer screen, I was studying the files on a disk labeled COLUMNS-'85–'90.

The file name GUN.TXT nudged me, and I called

it up, and saw the title, "Gun Mall," a hard-hitting discussion of the ease with which our local youth can lay their tender hands on firearms.

I copied the file onto my hard drive, brought it up again and launched a quick rewrite that began with a new title, "Johnny Got a Gun," and a change of the date, and some minor updating of information. Not much had changed in seven years—stone lions continued to crouch in front of the Art Institute, and the Board of Trade was still hopping.

The opening paragraph and the closer were brand new. Nothing unethical about it. After all, recycling is the new American way, right?

I typed "30", gave the "save and print" command and sighed contentedly.

"Another hard day at the office," I said. "Time to go home."

I slipped into my trenchcoat, ambled out into the city room, three pages of copy in hand, still hot off the laser printer; I was looking for Matt Greenfield. I wasn't the only one.

Betty Hargis, the wire editor, a slender woman with substantial talent, was leaning over a flashing screen at the city desk computer. Screens in a newsroom don't flash like that unless it's a bulletin.

"Matt!" she was calling. "We got a bullet!"

Then I saw Greenfield emerging from the men's room. I was crossing to him to give him the column, but he was moving quickly to the city desk and that flashing screen.

"AP news alert," Hargis said.

" 'Midrail Train #417 Derails,' " Matt read aloud. " 'Fatalities.' Where the hell's Shapiro?"

I was standing nearby, rocking on my heels, like a school boy waiting to turn in his homework.

"She went home," Hargis said, shrugging.

"What about Knobloch?"

"Covering the fire in Winnetka."

Matt turned and gazed around the newsroom, looking for a warm body. I was cinching my trench-coat when his eyes landed on me; his expression was at first irritable—so I stepped out of the way, so he could see behind me. But when I moved, his gaze followed me and his frown became a smile.

"Didn't you used to be a reporter?" he asked slyly.

"You can't be serious." I handed him the column. "Here. Right on time."

"Where's Jake?" Matt said.

He wasn't talking to me; he was asking this of Suzie, his secretary.

"Home with a 103 temp, Mr. Greenfield."

"Tell my secretary to get me Varney, at home. Or Kovler—he lives out that way."

"Yes, sir," Suzie said, and scurried off.

Matt, still standing near the city desk and the flashing computer, began to quickly check my column. I rocked on my feet some more. Out of my office came my ever-efficient secretary, with three-hundred-dollars worth of new loafers in one hand, and a battery-powered electric razor in the other.

"You have a dinner party to go to, remember?" Jeannie said. "At Barry Axler's in Oak Park?"

"Shit! I almost forgot."

I sat on the edge of a nearby desk and changed my shoes. Then Jeannie produced a mirror from somewhere (she could do her share of magic tricks, too) and held it up while I shaved.

"You got the address?" I asked her.

She handed me a slip of paper. "I made a map."

"I'm bad with maps."

"A child could follow this one."

I shrugged. "Then I'll take a child along. When's cocktail hour?"

"Seven-thirty," she said. "And don't forget *Good Day Chicago* tomorrow morning—Andrew Greeley's the other guest."

"Who's on first?"

She smiled. "You don't pay me enough to play Costello to your Abbott. Just don't be late. Those shows sell books."

"Well, I hope the host has *read* the book this time."

"I asked, and they said she'd listened to the audio cassette."

"Familiarity with an abridged version is better than no familiarity at all. I guess."

Matt was saying to his secretary, "Varney's wife is having a baby? Does she have to do it on *his* time? What about Kovler?"

"I got a feeling I better leave," I said, handing Jeannie the shaver.

"Kovler's not home?" Matt said. "Did you check with Jake?"

" 'Bye," I said to Jeannie, and she waved, and I moved quickly.

But not quickly enough.

"Jake's fever is up to 104?" Matt was saying. "Brackett!"

I kept moving.

"*Brackett!*"

I didn't turn around. "I'm not a reporter any-more, remember? I haven't worked the police beat since Irv Kupcinet was covering fires."

"And I'm not *Nick at Nite*."

Now I turned. "What's *that* supposed to mean?"

Matt did the Spock-eyebrow trick again. "The *Chronicle* doesn't print reruns."

I walked toward him, working up some indignation along the way; it felt pretty genuine by the time I got to him.

"I don't believe what I'm hearing," I said. "Are you accusing me of self-plagiarism?"

"Certainly not," Matt said.

"Well, that's better."

"I feel ashamed."

"You should."

"I feel bad. If you had, you'd be in violation of your contract, and . . . well. Tell you what. We'll just pull your columns up from the mid-eighties, and have a look. Something like, 'Gun something,' 'Son of a Gun.' I'll put a copy boy on that. . . ."

I turned to Jeannie, who had witnessed this farce.

"Call Barry Axler," I said, "and tell him I might be a little late."

A searchlight from a hovering fire-department helicopter threw light on the ghastly spectacle; from up there, this might look like a single car from a toy train, fallen off its tiny track. Close up, the remains of the last car on Midrail 417 was a collage of crushed wood, glass, and steel, with the occasional splash of blood. It was not difficult to imagine what the people in there might look like now, particularly not when you could see paramedics loading the bodies into the zippered bags, then carrying them into the nearby open field.

What the hell was *I* doing here? A cool fall evening, under a beautiful dark blue sky, with a scattering of glittering stars and an art-deco slice of moon—a hell of a night to get waylaid. Of course, my being late to a dinner party didn't quite compare to this train-carload of people who *really* didn't get where they were going.

I had almost forgotten the circuslike atmosphere of a disaster scene like this—police cars, ambulances, fire engines, their lights flashing and whirling hypnotically, news vans, and the ever-present churning of the overhead chopper, its light searching the wreckage. Workers in hard hats and goggles were trying to torch the rear door of the crushed beer can of a train car, their acetylenes burning blue in the night. We were out in the country, but there was a horde of spectators behind the police barricades. Nothing brings them out like a train wreck.

But at least these citizens didn't make a buck doing it, like I did. I felt like a relic of another time, with my spiral notepad, in the midst of minicams and live TV stand-ups. I moved past a pile of luggage, spotted our photographer on the scene, who was doing his best to capture the entire panorama in a single pop of a flashbulb.

"Andy," I said.

"Jesus, Pete Brackett! What are *you* doing here? Since when do they send the first team out on *this* kind of duty?"

"I think it's more like scraping the bottom of the barrel. Can you point me to somebody worth talking to?"

"I think so. There's an eyewitness, and nobody's talked to him yet."

"How they'd miss him?"

"He was on the car next to the one that got derailed. The cops have him. Over there. . . ."

The kid—well, to me he was a kid, though he

was probably twenty-two—was named Tim Weiss. He was wearing a tuxedo.

"We came straight from the reception," he said. He was in shock; apparently uninjured, but in shock just the same, with the frozen eyes that go with the territory.

He and his bride, Amy, had been on their honeymoon. The kid had a police blanket around his shoulders. I took notes as he told his story. Finally, it got interesting.

"I was on my way back from the club car when I heard it."

"Heard what?"

"A sort of a . . . loud sound. A clank. Then there was this jolt."

"What'd you go to the club car for, Tim?"

"Uh . . . we were out of champagne."

"I see. What happened, then—after you heard the clank?"

"Well, the jolt knocked me on my butt. When I got back on my feet, I went to the rear door and saw that the next car, where I was headed back to . . . the one with Amy still on it . . . it'd got loose, and was goin' wildly back down the hill." He touched his forehead, the glazed eyes widening. "God, it was really flyin'. . . ."

Three men were walking straight toward me, like cops about to make an arrest; but they weren't cops. It was three men in Midrail windbreakers—a couple security guys and Kenny Bacon, head of Midrail P.R. Kenny was a dark-haired, round-faced intense guy about my age. I knew him from way back—he was a fixture in the Chicago media scene.

And he was no dummy.

Neither was I: I had latched on to the only

eyewitness, and I wanted him on ice before any other reporters got wind of him. A TV camera crew was looking our way—I'd been recognized, and it wouldn't take long for them to figure out I wasn't talking to a nobody—so I had to move.

The kid was weeping, now—a good sign, actually. Maybe the shock was wearing off. I took him by the arm and walked him gently toward the approaching trio from Midrail.

"Kenny," I said.

"Pete," he said.

I leaned toward him and whispered, "This kid's had enough for one night. You want to keep him in one piece, I'd get him off the firing line."

Bacon looked at me hard; then he nodded.

"Thanks," he said, but there was at least some faint sarcasm in it. He knew I'd already got something out of the kid.

Bacon's two assistants hustled the groom away as Kenny stepped in where the TV crew, smelling blood, was moving in.

"No more questions," Bacon told them, motioning to some nearby cops, who stepped in to block the way.

Me, I had my story, so I smiled and saluted my colleagues from TV-land, and was heading up to the roadside where I parked my car, when I smelled something, and it wasn't fertilizer.

In fact, it was Chanel No. 5.

I have more than a few weaknesses, and that particular fragrance, wafting through the night air, is definitely one of them.

I glanced back and saw only a nest of hard hats working on the upended train car, their blowtorches glowing. But down among the heavy workboots was an unlikely sight: a pair of sleek, black stiletto heels with just the right sort of sleek, gracefully muscular legs that went with them. A well-turned calf is another of my weaknesses, so I studied the situation further.

She bent down into sight, this girl—woman, *young* woman (I have neckties older)—picking something up from the damp, dark grass. Then she moved away from the group of workmen, stepping out to hold that something up to a searchlight. Something small.

She stood silhouetted against the incandescent white light, frozen for several long moments, a living work of art. Then she stepped out into the night, where she was clearly just your everyday, average, dazzlingly beautiful young woman.

And even as she frowned at whatever it was she was studying, she displayed features so pretty, so delicate, they took my breath away.

On the other hand, it hasn't been that long since I quit smoking, so a lot of things take my breath away.

Andy sauntered up next to me, in the process of packing away his gear.

"Who's the dish?" I asked.

"You dog," Andy said. "You're the third guy who's asked me that tonight. *I* never saw her before, either."

"Damn."

"But I hear she works for the *Globe*. You leavin'?"

"Uh . . . no. No. I better stick around and see if Bacon gives a press conference."

"You dog," Andy said, and grinned.

3

My First Scoop

BYLINE: Sabrina Peterson

It was so shiny it winked at me in the grass; so small, I had to poke around looking for a while, but then I found it, plucked it from the wet grass, and held my prize up to the light.

A ring: a wedding band.

I tried it on my own fourth finger of my left hand—first time I'd put a ring on that finger since my own brief, but not-brief-enough, marriage. The band fit me snugly, so I knew it had belonged to a woman passenger.

Then I remembered seeing the young man in the tuxedo, whom the police had hustled into a squad car. If this ring belonged to a bride, could he have been her groom?

I glanced around, but the first thing my eyes landed on was another pair of eyes staring at me. Light blue eyes, a little small for the lantern-jawed face. His expression was blank, and not as openly lustful as some men who size you up.

And, frankly, I'm fairly used to being sized up. I don't mean to sound arrogant (I'll leave that to someone else), but I've always been pretty, and sometimes it's been pretty annoying. Men stare and sometimes fawn, and women can be resentful.

But if they get to know me at all, they find out I have a fairly respectable brain, and then can forget about the "pretty girl" nonsense and treat me like a human being.

I couldn't tell if Peter Brackett—and this *was* Peter Brackett staring at me, I recognized him at once, as would anyone in the Chicago area who wasn't sight-disadvantaged, so prevalent were the posters of that smug puss of his—was sizing me up as a "pretty girl" or as a fellow reporter.

Maybe it was a little bit of both.

At any rate, I did my best to keep my expression as blank as his—I didn't want him thinking I was impressed by seeing a celebrity, or that I was thinking of him as a hunk, which to tell the truth he was and is. I try to avoid reverse sexism.

So I looked away from him, just as he was averting his own gaze, and spotted the squad car parked on the grass, away from the hubbub. The young man in the tuxedo was in the back, and no cops were keeping him company, either inside the vehicle or out. I smiled, closed my fist over the ring, and stepping across a body bag, headed toward the cop car.

But as I approached, a uniformed officer walked

into view, a heavy-set suburban cop, who leaned his considerable weight against the hood of the car, sipping the coffee in a paper cup he'd left his post for briefly. With him standing guard, my interview subject might as well have been hermetically sealed.

"Judy," I called.

Judy was the *Globe*'s photographer, who'd been sent along with me on the story. She was an attractive redhead with an eye for composition.

"I got some decent shots," Judy said, loading up her film. "You having any luck?"

"I think I'm going to," I said. "See that cop over there? The one that seems to be wishing he had a donut to go along with that coffee?"

"Sure."

"I wonder if he'd like to have his picture in the paper."

"Aw. I get you."

"I think he'd look striking with that crushed train as a backdrop."

"You're gonna go far in this biz, Ms. Peterson."

"That's the idea."

I waited for Judy to do her thing—and it wasn't hard, the cop beamed, but demurred for a second, then looked around to see if any of his superiors were watching, and shrugged, allowing his vanity (and Judy's nice smile and red hair) to get the better of him.

Once Judy had led him away, I tapped on the window of the squad car. The young man in the tuxedo looked up, startled out of his glum reverie. He had been crying.

I showed him the ring through the window and his reddened eyes got large.

He unlocked the back door of the squad car and allowed me to slide in next to him.

"My name's Sabrina Peterson," I told him. "I'm with the *Globe*. What does this ring mean to you?"

"It's Amy's," he said, and he began to weep.

I comforted him, and then he told me his name was Tim Weiss and that's how I became one of two journalists in Chicago to land an interview with the sole eyewitness.

And Peter Brackett didn't get the juicy quotes I did.

Half an hour later, with the overturned train car as a gruesome backdrop, a priest with a booming voice did his best to fill the out-of-doors cathedral of the nighttime.

"If I could have your attention, please!" he called. His Bible was in his hand. "I wonder if everyone might pause in their labors to join me in prayer."

I was still taking notes. I hadn't wanted to spook Tim Weiss, and waited till after I'd had my brief-but-telling interview with him, to write it down. I have a near-photographic memory, which can come in handy: sometimes a notepad or mini-recorder makes a subject awkward. Better to seem to be just having a conversation with an interviewee, as long as you can quote them accurately later on.

Anyway, I was jotting down my notes as the squad car with the groom in back pulled up off the grass onto the highway and, lights flashing, drove into the night. I could feel eyes on me, and I glanced up, and Peter Brackett was watching me, frowning. Had he seen that I'd gotten an interview with Tim Weiss?

The workmen and the media reps were gathered

around the priest, an unlikely conglomeration of blue-collar and white-collar types, but a disaster like this is a great leveler. You don't think about any status but your own as a human being when you're surrounded by zippered body bags.

To tell you the truth, I was about the only person who wasn't praying; I was busy transcribing. I glanced up to see if Brackett was still watching me, and he wasn't, but I noticed something odd.

One man at the edge of the crowd, near the train—a tall, thin man with cadaverous features, wearing a khaki suit—was slowly scanning the perimeter. He almost made me shudder. His sunken cheeks and piercing gaze made me think of a vulture about to munch on some carrion.

Somebody else was taking advantage of the prayer-in-progress. Two teenagers, male, wearing gang-type jackets, ran out of nowhere, plucking several suitcases and at least one briefcase off the pile of salvaged luggage that was stacked to one side.

You almost had to admire their efficiency. They had struck, and run to their beat-up old Pontiac, waiting with its lights off in the field nearby, and rumbled off before anyone had noticed.

Well, almost anyone. I had noticed.

And I think the cadaverous-faced thin man had seen them, too. In fact, he was looking in the direction they'd disappeared, frowning.

The priest concluded his prayer, but before the crowd of workmen and reporters broke up, Midrail P.R. man Kenny Bacon stepped up and lifted a bullhorn and delivered his own benediction.

"Ladies and gentlemen," he said, his voice distorting and crackling, "at the present time, we're attempting to piece together the chain of events that led to the derailment of Midrail's 417. From what we've been able to ascertain, the last car decoupled at approximately five-twenty P.M., traveled down this incline, where it derailed and overturned."

"How many fatalities?" called out a WGN newswoman.

The Chicago media knew an impromptu press conference when they saw one.

Bacon lowered the bullhorn, and raised his voice. "There are five known fatalities. Those names will not be released until their respective families have been notified."

Another reporter yelled, "What about injuries?"

"We don't have a number on that. We hope to have a more formal press conference tomorrow morning. . . ."

I was talking to myself via note taking, a longstanding habit, and had just scribbled the question I would ask—*Who serviced the train???*—when somebody next to me spoke.

"They're not going to tell you."

I looked up and Peter Brackett was standing next to me. His smile in that rugged, rumpled face was a little smug, but not really unkind.

"Pardon me?"

"They're not going to tell you who serviced the train. Don't bother asking the question."

"Why?"

"Why aren't they going to tell you, or why shouldn't you bother asking?"

"Both," I said tightly.

"Well, they're not going to tell you because they want to talk to whoever-it-is-that-serviced-the-train before you or I or any of these other distinguished members of the Fourth Estate."

"I don't see how it can hurt to ask."

"It always hurts to ask a question that you *know* they won't, they *can't*, answer. You gotta swim in this media stream every day, kid. Why piss 'em off?"

Well, he was pissing *me* off. I raised my hand as high as the smartest girl in class, who just knew she had the right answer.

Bacon acknowledged me, pointing. "Yes . . ."

"Sabrina Peterson from the *Globe*," I said, putting some volume in my voice. "Do you have the name of the employee who serviced the train last?"

Bacon's face went tight and his eyes turned cold. "That information isn't presently available."

"Well, then," I pressed on, "could you tell us . . ."

"Yes—Cynthia!" Bacon said, ignoring me, pointing to someone else.

I could feel Brackett looking at me. I didn't look back. I didn't want to give him the satisfaction.

"First day on the job?" he asked.

I still didn't look at him. "No, this isn't my first day on the job!"

"Second?"

Bastard. I hoped my expression didn't tell him he'd guessed it right.

Now he was trying to turn on the charm.

"I know I'm right, or close to it," he said, " 'cause if you'd been in town longer than a couple of days, I just *know* we'd have met."

Jesus!

I turned and gave him the coldest, male ego withering stare I could muster.

He just took it in stride, holding out his hand. "Name's Brackett. Peter Brackett."

Like he was saying Bond, James Bond. What incredible arrogance!

"I work for the *Chronicle*," he said.

"Oh, really?"

"Where are you from, Peterson?"

"Podunk, obviously. You know, I realize every cub reporter in a skirt must get all trembly at the thought of meeting the illustrious Peter Brackett. But I happen to take my job seriously and, frankly, I can't believe you're hitting on me in the middle of a goddamn press conference at a *disaster* site!"

"Hitting on you? Is that what you think I'm doing? You must have a pretty high opinion of yourself."

"Well, I guess you're kind of an expert in that area, aren't you? Look. Let's get something straight: You have no chance. Zero. Trust me. You're just wasting your time."

"Is *that* what you were looking for in the grass?"

"What?"

"Your Midol?"

I should have slapped him, but, damn it, he had this twinkle in those little bitty blue eyes that took the edge off, and he damn near made me laugh. The bastard.

"Santa Rosa *Gazette*," I said.

"What?"

"That's where I'm from. Santa Rosa, California. That's the paper where I learned my trade."

"Oh. So working for the *Globe is* a step up."

I smirked. "Maybe the *Globe isn't* the *Chronicle*, but I happen to think you can't really call yourself a newspaperman until you've worked Chicago."

"A newspaper*man*?" He arched an eyebrow,

smiled one-sidedly and gave me a quick once-over.
"In spike heels?"

"Last question," Bacon was saying.

Damn! He had distracted me through the greater
part of the press conference.

I blurted out, "I understand there was a 'black
box' on the train! If so, will that tape be made
available, and when?"

Next to me, Brackett chuckled and shook his
head. "Hang in there, Peterson."

He ambled off, as Bacon was reluctantly answering my question.

"Yes, there was a data recorder, Ms. Peterson,"
the P.R. man said, "but when it will be available, I
can't at this time say."

Then Bacon nodded over to one of his assistants,
who was hanging up a mobile phone, giving his boss
a discreet nod. *Something had just been fixed.* I hadn't
been in Chicago long, but I knew enough to know
about fixing. . . .

But, what?

The Midrail Building in downtown Chicago was
across the river, beyond the Merchandise Mart, a
glass-and-steel tombstone decorated with the distinctive Midrail logo. The blue, late-model Chrysler
pulled into the building's nearly empty parking lot,
came to a stop, and Kenny Bacon got out on the
rider's side, and the assistant I'd seen him nod to,
got out from behind the wheel.

I had followed them here from the disaster site,
and was now parked across the street in my three-
year-old red Saab (wishing I had chosen a more
discreet color for my wheels).

Bacon and his assistant moved toward the building, and then two people who had been standing near the side wall, a man and a woman hidden in the shadows, stepped into view.

The man was lanky, wearing a work shirt and jeans, smoking a cigarette nervously; the woman was a blonde in a plaid shirt and jeans. They had a blue-collar look—they were people who had listened to country and western before it got fashionable.

A security guard met Bacon at a side entrance, and the P.R. man led the lanky man and the assistant inside. The guard disappeared inside, as well.

That left only the blonde, who was lighting up a cigarette for her own round of nervous smoking. She made her way to a Bronco that was one of the few cars, other than the Chrysler, parked in the Midrail lot at this time of night.

What the hell.

I got out of the Saab, jogged across the street, and approached the woman with a smile.

"Hi."

The blonde seemed startled, and almost dropped her cigarette. She was pretty, but a little hard. I guess she'd led a pretty hard life.

"Sorry," I said. "Didn't mean to scare you."

"What do you want?" Her voice had some gravel in it; this wasn't her first cigarette. Her eyes were wary, and a little red. Had she, like Tim Weiss, been crying?

"I'm Sabrina Peterson." I extended my hand. "I work for the *Globe*."

The woman ignored my hand, swallowed, and looked up at the looming Midrail building.

"It's okay," I said. "I already talked to Mr. Bacon at the crash site. Were you there? Were you on the train?"

"No. We, uh . . . just heard about it on TV."

"I see."

"Then, uh . . . we got a phone call." She looked away.

I had a hunch.

I leaned against the Bronco, but didn't crowd her. "You know," I said, "I can really sympathize with the guys that serviced that train. I hate to think of anybody blaming them . . . accidents like this, they just *happen.*"

"Yeah, well, how would *you* like to get a call saying a train you worked on just derailed and killed five people?"

Bingo.

"That would be rough . . . but blame is like credit, right? You have to share it. Surely there were *other* people involved in checking that coupling that came undone."

"No there weren't," she said. She shook her head, her expression bleak. "No ma'am. Not on this train. There was just one."

"One? Who?"

"My husband," she said.

The newsroom of the *Globe* is a cramped, funky place, and in the wee hours after midnight, it's staffed pretty much by a skeleton crew. But I found my city editor, Rick Medwick, in his small office, pounding away at his computer keyboard.

"Are you still here?" I asked him.

"Maybe I came in early." Rick grinned. He is young for a city editor, rumpled, harried, his dark hair thinning. "What's up?"

"I think I got a scoop."

His grin widened. "On your second day?"

"On my second day."

He went over to his computer printer to check something he'd just printed out. "Well, trust me, we can use it—I was just going over our latest market research, and we're down another six points."

"Papers are doing poorly all over the country, Rick."

Not the *Chronicle*. They're *up* nine points."

I rolled my eyes. "Now I know why you're raiding the Santa Rosa *Gazette* for talent."

"What have you got? Is it the train crash?"

"Sure is. A name. Ray Boggs."

"Who the hell is Ray Boggs?"

I sat on the edge of his desk. "The worker responsible for checking that coupling."

Rick's eyes got bright. "No one has this name but you?"

"That's right." I told him how Bacon at the impromptu press conference wouldn't cop to who was responsible for checking the coupling, and how I'd followed him to the Midrail Building, where they had taken Boggs up to their office, leaving his wife in the parking lot for the taking.

"Unfortunately," I said, "after I got her husband's name out of her, she got nervous. She clammed up, and then somebody was coming out of the building, and I split."

"The better part of valor," Rick said.

"I know I can get more out of her if I can get her on the phone. How do I run Boggs on the data base? I want to check up on this guy, and get his wife's number so I can try again."

The brightness in Rick's eyes dimmed; he was clearly embarrassed. "The data base system was shut down three percentage points ago. We're looking for something cheaper that the board of directors will approve."

"No problem. I'll just use the Santa Rosa data base."

"What's that?"

I grinned and sighed. "The phone book."

I tried fourteen names—who the hell knew there were so many "Boggs" in the world, let alone the greater Chicago metro area? The spiel was always about the same.

To the women who answered: "Mrs. Boggs, this is Sabrina Peterson with the Chicago *Globe*. Sorry to call so late, but I was wondering if by any chance you were related to the Ray Boggs who works for Midrail?"

To the men: "Mr. Boggs? Good evening, sir, or rather, good morning . . . this is Sabrina Peterson with the Chicago *Globe*."

The responses varied. People swear at you a lot when you call them in the middle of the night. Quick hang ups, and even the occasional polite response. Sometimes they said they already subscribed before slamming the phone down.

I was getting tired. I opened a bottle of apple juice as I tried again.

A woman's voice answered. "Yes?" She sounded older than the blonde I'd spoken to in the Midrail parking lot.

"Mrs. Boggs, this is Sabrina Peterson with the *Globe*—"

And that was as far as I got. The click startled me, it came so fast.

I punched redial.

"Yes?"

"Mrs. Boggs, I think we got cut off."

"What do you want?"

I sipped the juice. "Mrs. Boggs, are you related to the Ray Boggs who works for Midrail?"

There was a long pause.

Then the woman said, "Yes . . . he's my son."

I about did an apple-juice-spit take. "Mrs. Boggs, are you aware of the train crash tonight?"

"I saw it on the news. Then I called Ray."

"Why did you do that?"

"Well. I was afraid."

"Afraid?"

"That it might . . . I shouldn't say this."

Was she crying?

"Might what, Mrs. Boggs?"

"Be his fault."

"Why would it be his fault, Mrs. Boggs?"

"You know. His drinking problem."

4

War

—

BYLINE: Peter Brackett

I had exited WFLD-TV on North Michigan Avenue, collected a peck on the cheek from my publicist, Lindy, and was heading south, enjoying the mild lake breeze, when I passed a corner newsstand where a female Yuppie in a business suit was asking, "Do you have the *Globe*?"

The reply—"Sorry lady, sold out!"—was as unexpected as the question.

The *Globe* was the also-ran in this town. What a bizarre exchange. . . .

At the next corner another newsstand was doing a brisk business, and I did a double take noticing customers eagerly glomming onto copies of the *Globe*. The stack of unsold, unwanted *Chronicles* nearby wasn't as tall as the Sears Tower, but it was a close call.

Was I on *Candid Camera*? I thought they canceled that show an eon or two ago. . . .

But as I walked along, everywhere I looked, Chicagoans were greedily gobbling up the *Globe*: a guy gliding by in the window of a passing bus (with my own self-satisfied face looking back at me from the side-panel billboard), a woman at a table at a sidewalk cafe, a barber seated in a lawn chair in front of his shop. One and all eagerly devouring the *Globe*.

Who the hell was I to argue with the public?

In an effort to take said public's pulse, or test their sanity, I tossed a quarter on the newsstand counter and took the last *Globe*. I unfolded its tabloid front page and saw a picture of a cop with the crushed train car behind him.

Dumb picture.

The headline, however, was smarter: FIVE KILLED IN MIDRAIL CRASH—KEY RAILWORKER A PROBLEM DRINKER.

The byline, of course, was Sabrina Peterson.

The paper was tucked under my arm as I walked into the *Chronicle*'s city room. Nobody could look me in the eye, not even Jeannie, who I passed at a file cabinet she seemed to be trying to climb into. You would think these compatriots of mine would show some support, some sympathy, for someone about to die.

Last night, from the phone in my Cadillac, on my way to a fabulous dinner party at a fabulous Frank Lloyd Wright Prairie home in fabulous Oak Park, I had dictated my fabulous scoop—that is, my interview with groom Tim Weiss—to editor Matt Greenfield.

"That's pretty thin," he'd said.

"Maybe so, but nobody's gonna get anything else, 'cause there's nothing else to get. After I got my exclusive interview, Kenny Bacon clamped the lid on."

"You're sure about that?"

"Sure I'm sure. Jesus, now I remember why I grabbed the chance to write a column!"

Now I was standing in the doorway to Matt's office waiting for the inevitable.

" 'Nobody's gonna get anything else,' " he said, mimicking me mercilessly, " 'cause there ain't nothin' to get.' "

"I didn't say 'ain't.' I don't ever say 'ain't.' "

"Now I know *why* I made you a columnist. You're full of opinions, but *real* news is something foreign to your experience."

"Are you kidding? Just because an overzealous cub reporter, second day on the job—"

Both his eyebrows raised this time. "Well, that makes sense, then, her beating you out. She had inexperience on her side."

"She got lucky."

"She also got your 'exclusive' interview with Tim Weiss . . . only I like *her* quotes better."

I smirked. "Give me a break, Matt. I can out-scoop that kid any day."

His eyes narrowed. "Really?"

"Really."

"By tomorrow?"

"Why the hell not?"

He scratched his chin, smiled. "Care to wager?"

"How much?"

"Hundred bucks."

"You're on," I said.

Heading to my office, I again almost bumped into Evans, the obit girl. She had a solemn, somebody-died expression.

"I'm sorry about what happened . . ."

"Skip it," I said. "You want to help me back to my rightful position at the top of the heap?"

"Sure!"

"Then call the morgue and get me everything they have on this Boggs character. See if he has any friends, enemies, former wives, ever lost a job for any reason. . . ."

"You got it. I'll check the Nexus data base, too." She smiled and nodded and hustled off.

Jeannie was back to her desk in my office by the time I came in. She was finally about to offer her condolences when I shushed her.

"Get me the chief of police, the head of Midrail, the D.A., and call Sully and send him down to State Station, to sniff around."

Then I went back to Matt's office, stuck my head in and said, "Save me two columns above the fold, and I'd like my hundred in twenties, if you don't mind."

I came up with the scoop myself. All the fancy inside contacts in the world can't match a little shoe leather and a few sawbucks spread around to the right hourly workers. I spent the afternoon at the site of the accident, where hard hats were sorting through the rubble. A worker who had been scouting up and down the track came upon the missing coupling.

I got the first interview with him.

The worker's name was Rodriguez, and he was adamant about one thing.

"That coupling was *not* defective," he said. "We're talkin' human error, here, pal."

And I was talking scoop.

So I had some guys over for a poker game, and the night turned into morning, somehow. The sun was peeking in the windows when the phone called me away from a big hand with my bleary-eyed guests. I was winning, by the way.

"She did it again," Jeannie's voice said.

"Who did what when?"

"Spoken like a true reporter. Your friend, Ms. Peterson."

Or was I losing? "She didn't get my story, too, did she?"

"No. She got her own. You better run your fanny down to the corner newsstand. . . ."

And so there I was, Peter Brackett, award-winning columnist, a bona fide Chicago celebrity shuffling down Michigan Avenue, unshaven, looking half as good as your average homeless person, reading Sabrina Peterson's latest "exclusive" under the following headline: MIDRAIL #417 RAILWAY WORKER FLEES!

I was reading the story of Ray Boggs's disappearance for the third time when I entered the *Chronicle*'s newsroom, and a passing copy boy spoke to me. I didn't make out what he said the first time.

"I said, these just came for you, Mr. Brackett."

And he handed me a bright, colorful bouquet of flowers. It was like something the bride tosses to her chosen bridesmaid. Would I be the next to be married?

There was a card.

It said: *Not bad for four days on the job, huh?*

The signature was simply "S.P."

"Of course you know," I said to no one, "this means war."

Several evenings later, at the black-tie benefit of the gala opening of the Grant Wood exhibition at the Art Institute, I was well aware that the "war" between Sabrina Peterson and Peter Brackett was creating a buzz.

Earlier today, Matt Greenfield had paid me the two hundred dollars (a double-or-nothing variation on our original bet) and declared a moratorium on such wagering, declaring as well that my column be devoted to the Midrail affair, until further notice.

"I don't even care if you two keep trading scoops like this," Matt said magnanimously. "It creates interest."

"I heard the *Globe*'s circulation is up three points," I said glumly.

"Who cares? Ours is up two points, and we were way out in front to begin with."

Then on the way to the gala, I noticed a *Chronicle* delivery truck rolling down Michigan Avenue, with a new ad campaign and a fresh photo of yours truly: PETER BRACKETT—HE DELIVERS EVERY DAY IN THE CHICAGO *CHRONICLE*.

And just as I was feeling cocky about my restored prominence in local journalism, a *Globe* delivery truck rumbled by with Sabrina Peterson's sparkling, smiling face beside the banner: GET THE SCOOP, CHICAGO—READ SABRINA PETERSON TODAY!"

Maybe so, but "today" the scoop had been mine. Thanks to my sources at city hall, I had given the *Chronicle* the following exclusive: D.A. TO PRESS CHARGES AGAINST MISSING RAILWORKER.

And I sent rising-star Ms. Peterson a cardboard box with a puppy in it, lined with *her* latest scoop— LIQUOR FOUND IN RAILWORKER'S LOCKER—for house-training purposes. My sources at the *Globe* reported that upon delivery, the puppy urinated, as if on cue, all over Ms. Peterson's byline story.

Now, as I moved through the chic crowd in the museum's lobby, feeling suave in my tux, shaking the occasional male hand, bestowing a kiss on the occasional female cheek, I was beginning to get annoyed with cocktail banter on this one familiar subject. It was starting to be a pain in the ass, how many people wanted to josh me about my "feud" with Sabrina Peterson.

Then I spotted an old pal, Sam Smotherman, who had been a fixture around the Illinois political landscape for years. A small man with a big laugh, probably around my age, Sam had played roles rang-ing from lobbyist to campaign manager, fund-raiser to senatorial aide. With his curly dark hair and puppy-dog brown eyes, Sam fell short of handsome, but he was long on affable charm.

Right now he was holding court with a small group of rapt listeners who roared with laughter at an expertly delivered punchline. Sam was a self-admitted glad-hander, even a professional one, but he was damn good at it.

Sam noticed me, brightened, and broke away from the group, nabbing a caviar hors d'oeuvre off a passing tray as he approached me.

"Peter! How the hell's our bestselling author?"

"Don't try to convince me you've actually read

the book, Sam," I said, plucking a martini off another passing tray.

"I wouldn't kid a kidder," he said. "But I'm gonna listen to the tape, in the car."

I had to laugh. "Where'd you disappear to? I tried to call your office a few months ago, and the governor's staffers reacted like your name was a dirty word."

He snorted. "Tell me about it. I'm persona non grata these days—jumped parties."

"You? A Democrat?"

"No. Me, a capitalist. I'm working for Gayle Robbins."

"A woman boss? A chauvinist pig like Sam Smotherman?"

"Nonsense. I've always enjoyed working under women."

I sipped the martini. "No argument there. So you've left Illinois for Wisconsin?"

Gayle Robbins was a Wisconsin state senator who'd attracted some regional attention. She had a good reputation—a moderate Democrat who could pull Republican farm-country votes—so she was being groomed for a Washington bid.

"Couldn't resist," he said. "Gayle is a super lady. Bright. First-rate all the way."

He seemed sincere; but then, he always seemed sincere. It was his gift, and his profession.

Sam caught another hors d'oeuvre off a passing waiter's tray. "So, how about a sneak preview? Am *I* in your book? The dashing senator's aide who secretly slips the daring reporter the names of lobbyists offering kickbacks?"

"Afraid you didn't make it into *White Lies*. Maybe next time."

"You won't be sorry," he said, and this time he snagged a martini off a tray. "I'd make a good character, you know—bigger than life, charming, handsome . . ."

"Humble."

"But of course."

"You're definitely in the running for the sequel."

Sam's hearty laugh rose above the cocktail-party din. He deposited his empty martini glass on a tray. "So—what's the deal on this train crash? Does Midrail have its ass in a sling, or what?"

"Read my column."

"I've been meaning to, but lately the *Globe* has my attention."

"Traitor."

"She's prettier than you, Peter. And *her* writing isn't cynical."

I couldn't argue with that, either, so I grinned and tossed him a wave and headed for the bar. When I glanced back, he'd been joined by a statuesque brunette. She had big brown eyes, a lush mouth, and a Cindy Crawford mole.

If a political reprobate like Sam Smotherman could have a beautiful date for the evening, why couldn't the town's top columnist? But for the last week, since the "war" had started, I'd had the social life of a slug.

Just as I was luxuriating in this moment of self-pity, I noticed a woman at the bar. Her back was to me. One of the great dangers, and thrills, of being a man is seeing what seems to be a beautiful woman from behind. When she turns, will her face match the gentle curve of her back, the lovely porcelain skin exposed in the backless, black velvet evening dress? Will her features live up to the promise of the reddish-brown hair, worn stylishly up, and dangling pearl earrings?

I took a seat at the bar next to her. "Stoli," I told the bartender, "straight up."

Her lovely back was still to me.

The bartender served me, then said to her, "More champagne, madam?"

"Please."

She turned and held up her glass for him to refill it and it was her. We were damn near nose to nose: the *Chronicle* and the *Globe*.

"Hello, Peterson," I said.

My expression was blank. Hers, too.

"Hello, Brackett," she said.

We backed away and gave each other a little room.

"Taking the night off?" I asked.

"Put my story to bed hours ago."

"Me, too."

"Really? I look forward to reading it."

"You read the *Chronicle*?"

She shrugged. "I thought somebody still should."

I raised my tumbler, smiled a little, and she clinked the tumbler with her champagne glass, and smiled back a little.

"I've been reading you, too, Peterson."

"Oh?"

"Catching up."

She frowned faintly over the lip of her champagne glass. "Catching up?"

"I wanted to read some *vintage* Sabrina Peterson. The good stuff. Like, 'Zoo Transfers Feisty Gorilla.' Or 'School Bus Drivers Go On Strike.' "

She pursed her pretty lips in a smirk. "I'll take

that as a compliment, a journalist of your stature researching my early work."

"Well, it's very entertaining. You know what my favorite story of yours is?"

"No. Why don't you tell me."

I gestured in the air, painting a banner headline. " 'Pregnant Cheerleaders Reinstated.' "

She bristled a bit. "You can laugh. But that happens to be the story that made the wire services and got me my job at the *Globe*." She sipped her champagne. "By the way—thanks for the mutt."

"You're welcome."

"He's made quite an addition to my life."

"Hope you named him after me."

"Sort of. I call him 'Dick.' Synonym for 'Peter,' after all."

That made me smile, and I couldn't hide it. "Do you have to work at that smart-ass attitude, Peterson, or does it come naturally?"

"I picked it up," she said sweetly. "I've been reading your work since I was a little girl."

"Stop the presses!" somebody called. Somebody who seemed a little drunk. Somebody who was Police Captain Libro Taglianetti, a ruddy-faced, well-fed, streetwise copper in a tuxedo that was too tight twenty pounds ago.

"I've got a bulletin for you two," he said, the ice in his glass of Scotch clinking like dice being shaken.

"Spill," I said, hoping he wouldn't misunderstand and dump the Scotch on us.

"Guess who just showed up at the Central Station with a duffel bag and a yen to talk?"

"Ray Boggs!" I said.

But Peterson said it, too; we were in harmony, for once.

"What did he say?" I asked.

"He said," Taglianetti replied, then sipped his Scotch, "that he's innocent."

I set my drink down before I spilled it. Peterson was doing the same with her champagne glass.

"That ain't all," Taglianetti said. "He took a polygraph . . . it was his idea."

"And?" Peterson demanded.

"And he passed with flying colors."

I looked at Peterson and she looked at me; our expressions were stunned, our eyes wide as a flash-bulb popped, momentarily blinding us, making blinking fools of us both.

"What was that about?" she asked.

A freelance photographer had caught us in our first moment of truce.

"I think we just made the society page," I said.

5

We Do Lunch

BYLINE: Sabrina Peterson

Rick Medwick was drawing devil horns on Peter Brackett, who stood next to me in the picture on the *Chronicle*'s society page. My editor was sketching the horns on the photo as I paced in his small office.

"So according to the cops," Rick said, "Ray Boggs claims he had no idea where the bottle of liquor in his locker came from?"

"That's right."

"Never saw it before in his life."

"That's *ri*-ght."

Rick almost sneered as he leaned back in his swivel chair and gestured with two open palms. "Sabrina, the guy's a lush! He's got a history of . . ."

I pointed a finger at Rick—gently, as he is, after all, my boss. "Maybe so, but I tracked down his A.A. chapter. Boggs hasn't missed a meeting in three years."

Rick's eyes narrowed as he gently rocked in the chair. "You don't actually think the poor bastard is innocent?"

"That's a good question. If this 'poor bastard' is innocent, and Midrail rules out both mechanical and human error . . . what does that leave?"

Rick stopped rocking. His eyes were wide now. "Murder?"

"Wouldn't *that* be an interesting wrinkle?" I said, allowing myself a smile. It may seem ghoulish, but murder probably makes a lot of reporters smile, if it turns up in the right instance.

And this was certainly the right instance.

"Maybe Ray Boggs isn't the story at all," I said. "Maybe he's a red herring somebody has thoughtfully fitted for a frame."

My melodramatic phrasing made Rick smile.

"Maybe you attended one too many film noir festivals out in California," Rick said.

"Are you saying this isn't worth pursuing? Are you saying you wouldn't like me to keep this story on the front page of the *Globe*? Are saying you don't want to see the circulation points keep rising?"

"No," he said, with a tight little smile. "I'm not saying that."

I leaned across his desk. "Well, are you saying I should go down to State Street Station, and see if somebody down there saw something that day and never thought of mentioning it? Are you saying we oughta make sure the city of Chicago isn't about to lynch a guy for something he never did?"

"Yes," Rick said. "That's exactly what I'm saying."

And he drew a mustache on Peter Brackett's puss.

But I didn't get anywhere at State Street Station. I talked to redcaps, conductors, a waitress in the coffee shop, a bartender on a train between stops, an engineer, a shoe-shine person. Several of them told me that Peter Brackett had been around asking the same, or at least similar, questions.

Our paths didn't cross, but I could only hope he had come up as empty as I had.

I'd been meaning to talk to Tim Weiss again, but his bride Amy's funeral had been yesterday, and even a grasping reporter like yours truly has some feelings.

"How are you doing, Tim?" I asked him on the phone.

His voice, predictably, wasn't very steady. It was, in fact, a pained, halting whisper.

"It's tough, Ms. Peterson. It's . . . really hard."

"Tim, I'm still investigating the accident."

"Didn't . . . didn't that drunk who works for the train company cause it?" His voice tightened with rage. "I'd like to get that guy and—"

"Tim, there's a strong possibility Ray Boggs is innocent. He's been clean and sober for three years."

"But that doesn't make sense, Ms. Peterson."

"I know. I'm exploring a theory . . . and Tim, this is confidential, because frankly, it's a long shot, and it could make me look silly, if it does play out right."

"I understand. At least you're trying."

"Good. I'm glad you feel that way. I think . . . I think there may have been sabotage involved."

"*What?*"

"I know. It does sound absurd. Like I said, it's a long shot. But I need to know if you saw anything, or anybody, suspicious . . . either on the train, or perhaps at State Street Station when you were boarding."

"Ms. Peterson, I've gone over it in my mind, again and again . . . but I can't think of anything."

"Well." I sighed, but not into the phone. "Thanks anyway, Tim. If you do think of something . . ."

"The only thing . . ."

"Yes?"

"I didn't see anything suspicious, I was . . . too wrapped up in Amy."

He started crying. I could hear him. I waited. It took a while.

"The thing is," he managed, finally, "Dad got a lot of us at the train station, 'fore we got on."

"What do you mean, 'got a lot' of you?"

"On tape. You know, home-movie-type stuff. On his camcorder. Could that be helpful?"

Tim Weiss agreed to meet me at one-thirty at Murphy's Tavern in the Loop. It was another beautiful breezy day, and I walked from the *Globe* office on North Wabash, with my bulldog puppy, Little Dick, on a leash. I tied Dick up at a fire hydrant out front of the venerated newsman hangout. I wasn't worried about his safety—he had a growl beyond his years. His months, actually.

I'd come early enough to grab a turkey club sandwich and go over my notes. Near-photographic memory or not, I study my homework, more out of nervousness than necessity. I sat at the bar, nibbling my club sandwich, sipping my Perrier, when the empty stool next to me got filled.

"Well, Peterson! What a pleasant surprise."

I was getting to used to Peter Brackett's smirk. At least I was starting to understand that smirk was at least partly self-mocking.

"Small world," I said.

He tossed his spiral notebook on the bar between us. "Not so surprising, the city's top two 'newspapermen' would wind up here. This is a famous newshound haunt, you know."

"Really?"

"Sure. Speaking of hounds, that bulldog of yours tried to nip me outside. I just wanted to pet him."

"I've trained him well. So this is a well-known media meeting place, huh?"

"Absolutely, and long before they ruined it by calling us 'media.'" He glanced around affectionately. "Ben Hecht made this place his home away from home."

"Ben who?"

He looked at me with a mixture of pity and scorn; then he shook his head and said, "Just an old reporter back in the twenties."

"He was famous, huh? I'm betraying my ignorance."

"You're betraying your youth. And my age. He wrote *The Front Page*."

"Is that a book?"

He shook his head again. "I may cry. Ever see the old movie *His Girl Friday*?"

"Cary Grant? Rosaline Russell?"

He smiled. "You're starting to restore my faith in the younger generation." He leaned close. "Just a friendly word of advice: Don't let any other Chicago news types know you're not familiar with Ben Hecht. There's a little plaque with his name on it in the back booth . . . next to mine."

"Ahhh. Museum pieces."

His laugh was gravelly. "Score one for the younger generation. Hey, that sandwich looks good. What is it?"

"Turkey club on whole wheat, hold the bacon, hold the mayo."

He made a face. "You're eating a club sandwich *without* bacon?"

"Bacon is bad for you."

"So is getting hit by a bus, but a man's gotta cross the street sometime."

"But he doesn't have to cross with is eyes closed."

"I'll have a club sandwich myself," he told the bartender, "only with extra bacon and for God's sakes don't hold the mayo. And bring me a Coke."

The bartender went away, and I said to Brackett, "With that diet, you and Ben Hecht ought to be comparing notes before too very long."

"Speaking of notes," he said, with a sly grin, "you got quite a stack of 'em there yourself. You onto something?"

"You can find out tomorrow," I said, "for the price of a *Globe*."

The Coke came and a maraschino cherry was floating on top like an alien eyeball. Brackett picked it up by the stem and bit the red ball off and chewed merrily.

"Ugh!" I said. Now I made a face. "How can you *eat* that?"

"It's jaw action thing, followed by swallowing. I been doin' it for years."

"That's filled with Red Dye number three—

which stays in your system for thirty years. Not to mention that it's been linked to thyroid cancer."

He started to cough, and spit the remains of the deadly cherry into a cocktail napkin.

I sipped my Perrier. "Looks like you momentarily lost the hang of that jaw action/swallowing thing."

"You ever think of renting yourself out as an appetite suppressant, Peterson? Next time I go on a diet, I go nowhere without you."

The bartender arrived with the club sandwich, and Brackett said, "Shit! Forgot. I got a luncheon appointment!" He turned to me. "You got any change, Peterson? I gotta try to catch somebody on the phone."

"The money *you* make, and you're hitting a 'cub reporter' up for quarters?"

"Please."

"Okay, okay." I dug a quarter out of my purse for him, and he headed for the phone on the wall in the rear. He had left his spiral notebook behind. I was looking at it hungrily, thinking *Peter Brackett's notes, hold the mayo*, when there he was again, plucking the spiral pad from the bar, and smiling in my face.

"Nothin' personal," he said. "You got a pen I can borrow?"

"Jesus!" I said, but I gave it to him.

He gave me the smirk in return and headed back for the phone.

But he had inadvertently left something else behind: A small slip of paper, blank side up.

I stared at it for a while.

A tiny invisible devil appeared on my right shoulder and encouraged me to peek at the note. Then a tiny invisible devil appeared on my left shoulder and agreed.

I glanced over my shoulder. Across the tables of talking heads, he was lost in conversation on the phone, talking animatedly, his back to me.

I turned over the slip of paper. It was a phone-message memo from the *Chronicle*, and it said: "Sully found eyewitness confirming Boggs's innocence! Meet at end of Vantage Lane—Poplar Grove. 3 P.M. sharp." And it was signed "Jeannie" and dated today.

I checked my watch. Tim Weiss was due in half an hour, but if I waited for him, I wouldn't have time to intercept Brackett's eyewitness. And Brackett had a luncheon appointment he had to run to, so he sure wouldn't be early for his rendezvous in Poplar Grove. . . .

Brackett came back, told the bartender to put the club sandwich in a bag and give it to me.

"I gotta get over to the Tavern Club," he said, harried. "I really screwed up. Give that sandwich to some homeless person, would you? It's the politically correct thing to do . . . see ya in the funny papers, Peterson!"

He waved goodbye and all but ran out of there.

I wrote a quick note:

Tim—something important came up on the investigation. If you can, meet me at my office at the Globe around six p.m. If you can't, leave the tape with my editor, Rick Medwick.

I signed it, gave it to the bartender with a five-dollar bill and a description of Tim, ran out on the street, gave the sandwich in the bag to a street person, untied my pup, and we were gone.

6

All's Fair

—

BYLINE: Peter Brackett

Sabrina Peterson had a lot to learn about the news biz. Among the lessons that lay ahead for her were (a) convenient leads that seem too good to be true often are, and (b) five bucks isn't enough to properly pay off a Chicago bartender.

A Chicago cop, yes. In fact, you can get change, but that's another story.

That morning in my office, where I had tacked the society-page photo of Ms. Peterson and me to the dartboard for target practice purposes, I had met with my secretary Jeannie and my legman, Sully.

Jeannie had checked with the local A.A. and discovered that Boggs was currently a member in good standing; Sully had poked around Boggs's home neighborhood and interviewed his fellow workers and found them all in agreement: Boggs hadn't displayed his drinking problem in years.

Sully also discovered—in talking to these friends, neighbors and co-workers—that Boggs's attorney was lining up character witnesses from here to Gary, Indiana.

It was starting to sound like this poor schnook Boggs was innocent, and if he was, and if human error was not a factor, then maybe somebody had *caused* this disaster.

If this was a potential murder case, the place to start was where it all started: State Street Station. I went down and spoke to a dozen or more employees at the station, from waitresses to rest room attendants to the orange-uniformed workers who, like Ray Boggs, serviced the trains. Nobody had seen anything out of the ordinary.

"And *nobody* could have serviced that train after Ray Boggs?" I asked the unfortunate engineer of Midrail #417, whose first day back on the job this was.

"Not *that* afternoon," he said. He was a burly man with kind gray eyes and a face full of well-earned lines. "The guy who comes in after Boggs was sent out on a brake problem, on track seven."

"No other service people were working that track?"

"Not after four-thirty. That I can swear to."

By the time I got back to my office at the *Chronicle*, I was pretty well discouraged. It was almost lunchtime, but I didn't have much of an appetite.

But young Ms. Evans, of obituary fame, burst in all smiles, perking me up considerably.

Her eyes were bright. "I've been interviewing

passengers, right? Well, one of them remembers seeing Tim Weiss's *dad* taking a video of the bride and groom boarding the train."

I sat up in my chair. "A video? That's great!"

She winced. "Well—that's the good news."

"What's the *bad* news?"

"When I called Mr. Weiss, Tim's father, he said his son had an appointment after lunch with Sabrina Peterson."

"That's only bad news," I said, "if you don't know *where* they're meeting. . . ."

And Evans had smiled.

Which is how I wound up at Murphy's Tavern and managed to finesse Peterson into sneaking a look at the phony phone message that no doubt sent her scurrying off to Poplar Grove and an appointment with the little man who wasn't there.

Sad-eyed Tim Weiss had believed my story that I was working with Ms. Peterson now, and handed over the tape (a dub—"The original's very precious to me," Tim had said), and I hustled home to have a look.

My flat's in a gentrified neighborhood on the Near North Side—a big, comfortable upper-floor apartment, whose most noteworthy decorative note is the wall of shelves displaying my collection of antique typewriters from the twenties and thirties. One of them had belonged to Ben Hecht.

Old Ben wouldn't know what to make of my videotape and video-disc setup, let alone my several computers, both here and at work. Even now, I knew some writers (novelists, not reporters, who have all been forced to convert) who preferred the feel and bang of a Smith Corona. I agreed with them aesthetically, but sometimes technology was a plus.

I popped Tim Weiss's video into the machine, settled back in my easy chair, and began to watch, remote control in hand.

I had just begun when the phone rang, and I picked it up quick, reflexively, instead of doing the smart thing and letting the answering machine kick in.

"You simply must *not* be late," said a familiar nails-on-blackboard voice.

"Hello to you, too, Lindy."

"You better allow plenty of time. It's in Oak Brook, you know. The shopping center?"

"I know, Lindy."

"Rich clientele in that neck of the woods. They buy a lot of books."

"That's nice, Lindy."

"You don't want to get caught on the Eisenhauer."

"I sure don't. Don't fret—I won't be late, Lindy."

"Book signings are very important. Positive word of mouth is absolutely the best publicity. I don't mean to be a nag, but this is what you *pay* me for, my sweet, and when you don't take my advice, you're just throwing away your—"

"This time I'll be the first to arrive, and the last to leave. See you there."

I hung up. I'd been watching the tape as my publicist and I spoke, but nothing remarkable had shown itself as yet: Tim and the lovely, late Amy were waving at the camera; some school kids in the background were boarding the train. Then the camera lost focus, before zooming in on the newlyweds, who were throwing kisses to the camera as they boarded.

And the screen turned to snow.

For this I'd gone to the trouble of sending Sabrina Peterson to Poplar Grove?

Nonetheless, I kept replaying the tape in my mind as I tooled my Caddy onto the Eisenhauer Expressway. I'd left early, but hadn't missed rush hour. I kept going over it, turning off the amiable chatter on the LOOP radio station, wanting to concentrate.

The Rizzoli's bookstore was in a new section of the fashionable outdoor mall, off to one side, a very handsome two-story building. Lindy was out front waiting; she smiled and waved as I drew up alongside her. I let down the window on the passenger's side and called out to her.

"Just let me park this, and I'll be right there!"

"Great!"

"Wait a minute . . ." I wasn't talking to Lindy. "Shit!"

"What?" Lindy said, frowning, worried.

Then I was making a U-turn and speeding away, as Lindy ran out into the street after me, eyes wide, mouth agape. *Come back, Shane!*

But I was on my way back to Chicago, winding my way impatiently through the still heavy traffic, taking the shoulder when necessary. In front of my duplex, I squeezed into a parking space and flew up the steps. The tape was still in the machine. I grabbed the remote control, clicked the set on, hit "Rewind," then "Play."

I knelt in front of the TV as if accepting communion. I was so close the pixels weren't merging. I reared back.

There it was!

A man in orange! He was little more than a blurry orange blotch, but there he was. . . .

I rewound, hit "Slow play" and when the orange image came into view, I freeze-framed. I clicked the freeze-frame ahead, looking for the best still-frame image. Down in the corner of the screen, the time code said 5:07 P.M.

What was it the engineer at State Street Station had said?

Nobody had serviced that train after 4:30.

He could swear to that.

But that orange blur on the screen, as I clicked through the frozen images, became more and more obviously one thing: the uniform of one of the workers who serviced the trains.

The little man who wasn't there.

7

Palm Reading

BYLINE: Sabrina Peterson

It was after dark when I got home to my apartment in New Town, so pissed off I was boiling. I had the sack of no-MSG Chinese carryout in one hand, juggling my keys in the other, and Little Dick was under my arm, wriggling toward the bag of food, sniffing and whimpering wildly (the dog, not me!).

We—that is, Little Dick and I—had been sent on a literal wild goose chase by a certain *Big* Dick.

I'd fought expressway traffic, frantically trying to read an Illinois road map (transplanted Californian that I am), finding my way eighty miles into the heartland hinterlands to Poplar Grove, where at the end of a dirt road marked by a hand-painted sign that said VANTAGE LANE, I came to a dead end where wild geese were wandering around a little pond, clucking furiously.

I told you it was a literal wild goose chase, and Peter Brackett hadn't chosen this "address" randomly. He wanted to humiliate me, as well as steal my lead.

And steal my lead, I knew he had: I had stopped at a pay phone to call long-distance to the Weiss home and Tim's father told me that his son had given the videotape to my "associate," Mr. Brackett. My associate!

I placed the sack on my work-cluttered dining room table and removed the carryout cartons, while Little Dick jumped at my feet, nibbling at my slacks and whining pitiably, as if he hadn't already gone through two bowls of puppy chow today.

My apartment is modest, to say the least— bedroom, living room, kitchenette, and bath—with furnishings running to futons and modular stuff from Crate and Barrel on Michigan Avenue.

I fixed myself some decaffinated Constant Comment and flopped on the couch, put my feet up on the little oak coffee table and ate vegetable chicken out of the container with a spoon (I just wasn't in a chopsticks mood), feeding little scraps of fowl to my eager little pup. I sipped the hot tea, scowling at nobody, feeling sorry for myself. The phone on the end table next to me rang.

"Hello," I said, through a mouthful of Chinese.

"Is this Mrs. Peterson from the *Globe?*"

A young voice—male.

"It's Ms. Peterson, actually. Can I help you?"

I gave Little Dick a sliver of chicken.

"Um . . . my name's Danny Brown?"

Only a teenager in today's world could make his name a question.

"Yes, Danny?"

"Me and some guys were doin' some stuff . . . you know . . . at the train crash?"

I sat up. Little Dick was bugging me and I gave him a whole wonton and said, "What were you doing at the crash site, Danny?"

"You know. Looting?"

The back of my neck was tingling. "Go on, Danny."

"I didn't want to talk to the cops. Didn't wanna get in trouble."

"I understand that, Danny. Please go on."

"Well . . . I found somethin' in this briefcase. I don't exactly know what it is or means or anything, but I got a feeling it's important."

"Why, Danny?"

"I'd rather show you."

"Okay . . ."

"I mean, I know you been writin' about the crash in the paper a lot and everything, and figured you'd want to see this stuff. A friend of mine, he says you guys pay money for this kinda shit."

"Danny, that's exactly the kind of shit I'm in the market for. Where do you live?"

I'm new to Chicago, but I already knew Jackson Park had its high points—the Museum of Science and Industry, for instance, and the University of Chicago.

But the address in Jackson Park given me by Danny Brown was on what had to be one of the city's meanest streets, an array of decaying buildings, graffiti-stained walls and huddled homeless people. I parked in the red zone right in front of what had once been a magnificent movie palace, but was now just another public eyesore. Dreams had once flickered across the silver screen, here; now it was just another fading memory on a street of nightmares.

I stepped out of the Saab and immediately had a start, as the El rumbled by overhead. I caught my breath, clutching my purse as I walked to the graffiti-adorned, boarded up entrance of the old theater. The Yale lock on the one usable door was rusted and broken. I lifted it out of its hasp, opened the door, and stepped inside. I walked past the hollow eyes of cobwebbed ticket booths into a decrepit yet ornate foyer. Huge crystal chandeliers, their bulbs dimly flickering, guided my way.

I called out, "Hello! Danny?"

I swallowed, breathed deep, though the stuffy atmosphere in the once-grand foyer was hardly reassuring. I thought seriously about getting the hell out of there. Ahead was a curved, worn-carpeted staircase.

"Danny?"

I started up the stairs. On the landing I found myself in a makeshift warehouse of stolen goods: boom boxes, cellular phones, TVs, VCRs, cameras. In one corner, between stacked boxes and goods, was an equally makeshift "apartment"—a mattress with some blankets, a table, fridge, microwave.

A dog howled somewhere in the bowels of the theater, and I jumped. Somewhere a door slammed, and I quickly turned, even as its echo made the chandeliers shiver. Me, too.

Then I was catching my own reflection in a large, cracked wall mirror, but I saw something else as well, something, *someone*, stumbling up behind me. . . .

Where he came from, I wasn't sure.

But when I whirled, this teenager—who I felt sure was Danny Brown—was suddenly standing in front of me and between his eyes was a small, dark, irregular circle that I knew, somehow, though I'd never before seen one, was a bullet hole.

You can call me a coward; you can even call me a girl. But I screamed my bloody lungs out.

Then he pitched forward, into my arms, and I screamed some more. Louder.

I stepped back and the boy crumpled to the carpeted floor with a *whump*. I jumped away, and my foot must have caught the lamp cord, because the landing was plunged into blackness.

I didn't scream. I was past that. Whether in control, or shock, I couldn't say. Was someone besides Danny Brown up here with me? Had Danny toppled onto me, already dead, or was he pushed by somebody toward me, or what? How the hell should *I* know? I just got down on my hands and knees and fumbled around until I found the lamp cord, and then fumbled around some more and found the socket and plugged the thing back in.

I got up. I steadied myself against a wall of boxed VCRs, wishing I'd stayed in Santa Rosa with the pregnant cheerleaders.

This was a murder scene.

I didn't trust my fabled near-photographic memory for this one. I wanted to record every detail, and I fished around in my purse for my spiral pad and my pen. But I couldn't find the goddamn thing.

Shit!

Peter Brackett had my ballpoint pen! I'd loaned it

to him at Murphy's Tavern. I didn't know whether to scream, laugh, or cry.

Instead, I looked around for something to write with. There was a silver ballpoint pen on the floor, next to the dead boy, and that would do nicely, even if I did have to . . . oh, my . . . step over him to do so.

We will not discuss what the hole in the *back* of his head looked like.

Anyway, I was picking up the pen when I noticed them: the letters on the boy's left palm.

LD.

Two little letters, written hastily, with the very ballpoint I was reaching for. There was a smear, next to the LD, where a third letter might have gone.

This was a message he'd left either in his dying moments (did people shot in the head *have* dying moments?), or right before somebody shot him. Either way, this was what the detective stories called a dying clue!

I picked up the ballpoint, scribbled "LD" in my notebook and quickly went about the area wiping my prints off the lamp and anything else I might've touched.

Should I have called the police? Probably. But I was scared, and I was giddy, and I was confused, and every other emotion you can think of, except rational, and that isn't really an emotion. Shoving the notepad and pen in my purse, I ran down the stairway, through the foyer of lost dreams, out onto the street, and got in the Saab and took off, tires squealing, about as inconspicuous as a fire truck heading for a four-alarm fire.

I glanced in my rearview mirror and saw somebody standing across the street—was he watching me? A tall, thin man in a khaki suit, with a briefcase in his hand. Even though he was receding behind me, I could see that he had a scary, sort of cadaverous face.

Had I seen that face before?

And then I remembered: This was the man who hadn't lowered his head for the priest's prayer at the disaster site, who had instead been watching Danny Brown and his friends stealing luggage off the salvage pile.

Luggage, including a briefcase.

I had one further thought, and it went like this: *Shit!*

Then I hit the gas and was gone. I figured, if a cop stopped me, good.

8

Wish List

———

BYLINE: Peter Brackett

The view of the Chicago skyline from the windows encompassing the sixtieth-floor conference room of the *Chronicle* is undeniably breathtaking, particularly on a clear, late fall morning like this one. Equally undeniable was the fact that neither I, nor editor Matt Greenfield, gave a rat's ass.

We had other things on our minds, as we sat at one end of a conference table littered with more newspapers and empty Styrofoam cups than a state park on July fifth. Matt, in his shirt sleeves, tie loosened around his neck, brow furrowed as he chewed what once had been the eraser end of a Number Two pencil, was going over a legal-pad list of the victims from crash of Midrail #417.

"A butcher and his wife, a bride without her groom, an army recruiter," he said.

"A science teacher," I added, "and a shoe salesman. Not a likely murder candidate in the bunch."

Matt grunted, sat back in the chair, shook his head. "Maybe that's because there *isn't* one. Let's face it, Pete—just 'cause on that home-vid you glimpsed a railroad maintenance guy a few minutes *after* he was supposed to go off duty, that doesn't mean the #417 was rigged to kill one of these people."

"It's a classic technique," I said, with a shrug. "Hide your victim in a crowd of victims. Remember that 'serial killer' in '91, in Decatur, who bumped off five women 'randomly,' including his one true intended target, his better half?"

"Sure I remember, but like you said, there's not a likely victim *on* this list." He tossed the legal pad on the table and it landed with a little thud. "That's not exactly an index of America's most wanted, you know."

"Maybe not," I said, and finished my latest cup of coffee, "but I still say, this 'accident' is looking less and less accidental."

I reached for the legal pad, and tore off the list of names and addresses.

"I'll check 'em out," I said.

"You gonna put Sully on it? You want me to free up that girl from obits for you, too?"

"No. I'll run these names down personally. Then if I come up dry, it's my own damn fault."

I stood, tossed my crushed Styrofoam cup toward the wastebasket, the projectile bouncing off the rim. If Peterson had been there, I'll bet she'd have had a comment about my irresponsible behavior toward the environment.

"By the way," I said, about to go out the door, "that girl from obits is good. You should give her a shot."

He raised an eyebrow. "I'll keep that in mind. Smart young women are a hot commodity in the newspaper trade these days."

"Very funny."

I was almost out the door again when he called out and stopped me.

"Pete! Let me ask you something."

"You're the boss."

"Why are you sticking with this story?"

"Are you kidding? You said yourself, our circulation points are climbing."

"Sure, but the story's getting old, *and* cold. How many columns have you devoted to it already?"

"You're telling me? Every day I stay on this story, I lose money. I've been dodging calls from my editor, my agent, not to mention my publicist . . ."

"Then why the hell are you sticking with it?" He tossed his pencil onto the legal pad. "You're just grasping for straws now, don't you think?"

"Not straws. I have a genuine lead—a lead the competition doesn't have."

Matt grinned, and laughed, once. He locked his hands behind his head, fanning his elbows out, and beamed smugly at me as he leaned back. "I'm beginning to think that 'competition' is the best thing that's happened to this paper—and to *you*—in a very long time."

"Who am I to argue with my elders?" I said, and went out.

Finally.

* * *

For the next two days, I wore out more shoe leather
and tire treads than I had in the last five years of
writing columns. It felt good, at first, being a *real*
reporter again. But soon I remembered the frustra-
tions of real reporting.

Each interview began with a phone call—often
a number of phone calls, to home, to work, to
family—until I got an appointment nailed down with
the nearest living relative I could locate. Gradually I
crossed victims' names off the list, beginning with
Tim Weiss's lovely bride, Amy.

While I did all the interviews myself, I did have
some support: I put Sully on the insurance trail.
Even somebody as apparently heartbroken as Tim
Weiss might be delivering an Oscar–worthy performance if, say, a million dollars of life insurance was
at stake.

But according to Sully, who could root this kind
of thing out the way hogs find acorns, none of the
Midrail #417 victims was heavily insured, nor were
any of them wealthy enough for inheritance to be the
likely motive.

Slowly I was able to cross off the list the shoe
salesman, and the butcher, and his wife. By the time
I got to the U.S. Army Recruiting office on South
Clark, I had added "baker" and "candlestick maker,"
too, for the hell of it, crossing them out as well.

The recruiting officer was easily crossed off the
list—according to his superior, the late Sgt. John
McRae had been unmarried, with his next of kin a
younger brother in Alaska. I had crossed the sergeant
off the list, and was bending down for a drink of
water in the hallway, when the competition—looking

as professional as she was attractive in a pants suit—
stepped off the elevator.

Why the hell was *she* checking out the train-
crash victims?

I had kept my suspicions of murder out of my
column, wanting to keep this lead to myself for an
eventual bigger score. But here the esteemed Ms.
Sabrina Peterson was anyway, dogging my heels!

I didn't say anything to her, though. Maybe she
didn't see me there, bending over the water fountain.
She certainly gave no indication she'd noticed me.

Waiting until she'd gone into the recruiting office, I withdrew from my reportorial bag of tricks one
of the most time-honored of journalistic techniques.

I peeked through the keyhole.

And saw a lovely, brown, long-lashed female eye
looking right back at me.

"Son of a . . ." I said.

". . . bitch!" her muffled voice said, on the other
side of the door.

The science teacher's name was Beekman. He
lived—until the crash of the #417, that is—on a
quiet suburban street in quiet suburban Hinsdale.
Though it took several tries to get ahold of her, I'd
spoken to his widow this morning, and she'd con-
sented to an interview this afternoon.

Actually, it was almost dusk by the time I walked
up the walk to a modest ranch-style that had probably
seemed pretty spectacular in 1954. It still seemed
pretty spectacular to me, to tell you the truth, aging
baby boomer that I am. This neighborhood stirred
Howdy Doody memories in me. Wind rustled
through the leaves of a large oak with a kite was
stranded in its branches.

I rang the bell.

I stood for a while, listening to the soothing yet eerie whisper of the wind in the trees, then rang again. Finally an attractive brunette in her thirties, in a white blouse and black slacks, cracked open the door, tentatively.

"Yes?" she said.

"Mrs. Beekman? Peter Brackett, from the *Chronicle*. We spoke this morning?"

Her dark eyes flickered. "Of course."

"Thank you for returning my call, by the way. Not everybody bothers to do that."

"Mr. Brackett," she said edgily, and she slipped out onto the stoop and shut the door behind her. "This isn't a good time."

"I just have a few questions . . ."

"I'm sorry. I can't talk now."

Was she frightened?

She continued: "I don't want to talk about Mr. Beekman in front of the children."

That seemed an oddly formal way to put it.

"Well," I said, "I can come back tomorrow, when they're in school, or later tonight . . ."

"I have to work tonight." Her eyes were darting. "Can you meet me at my office?"

"Absolutely. When?"

"Nine. 1700 Walton, Suite 1864?"

"Sure. No problem. Mrs. Beekman—are you all right? Is something the matter?"

A dumb question to be asking a recent widow, but I blurted it out anyway.

"I'll explain tonight," she said and stepped inside, and then I was looking at the door.

And hearing it lock.

9

We Get the Shaft

BYLINE: Sabrina Peterson

The lake breeze that had been so pleasant the past several days had turned nasty tonight. It sent debris rustling down Walton Street, and the scarf around my neck whipped as I approached the high-rise office building.

The lobby was a well-lighted, high-ceilinged affair, and empty. My clicking heels echoed across it like little gun shots. Up ahead at the elevator, someone had just slipped on, as a cleaning lady was stepping off. I ran and turned the echo of my heels into machine-gun fire.

My hand stopped the elevator doors just in time, and they drew back for me, and I stepped on. The passenger who had beat me aboard was not a stranger.

"What the hell are *you* doing here?" he blurted, frowning. It was a hostile greeting, even for Peter Brackett.

The doors slid shut behind me.

"I could ask you the same thing," I said.

After all, what had he been doing the last couple days, checking the Midrail #417 victim list? Everywhere I'd gone, he'd either just been there, or was coming up behind me.

Only *I* could connect Danny Brown's murder with the train crash. What could he *have* that had led him into investigating the victims?

I certainly wasn't about to tell him that I'd had a call this afternoon from the science teacher's wife, Mrs. Beekman, asking me to meet her here tonight, in Suite 1864. I could hardly expect him to tell me if he had a similar appointment, which, damn it, I bet he had! Because the eighteenth-floor button was already lit up.

So neither of us said anything.

We just watched the elevator indicator as it informed us we were climbing, seven, eight, nine. He cleared his throat. I coughed. He scratched his thigh. Eleven, twelve. I smoothed out my slacks.

Then there was a jarring jolt as the elevator came to an unexpected, abrupt stop, well short of the eighteenth floor.

And the lights went out.

There is no darkness quite so complete and disturbing as the darkness of an elevator that has just come to a sudden, unwanted stop, a dozen stories up.

"Shit," I said, "this can't be good."

"Probably just a power outage. Wind's pretty fierce out there tonight."

His voice sounded calm, but I wasn't reassured.

"Shouldn't we *do* something?"

"You're probably right," he said.

Then I felt a hand on my chest. I batted it away.

"Sorry," he said, and sounded like he was. "I was just looking for the phone. There's always a phone in these things."

"Not under my blouse there isn't."

"I said I was sorry. Here it is!" he said.

I could hear him taking the phone off the hook. He didn't speak into it. All I could hear was him clicking the button, trying to get a dial tone, apparently.

"Dead," he said.

"The power outage, you think?"

"Well, the phone lines could be down, too, I suppose. But otherwise the phone would be working. It's not electrical."

We stood in the silence and darkness for several long moments.

"What are you doing here, Brackett?"

"What?"

"Did you have an appointment to meet Mrs. Beekman on the eighteenth floor tonight at nine?"

He paused, but just momentarily. "Yes. You, too?"

"Yes."

Another pause, then: "You think we've been set up?"

"You have a reporter's instincts, Brackett. I think we should try to find our way out of here, as fast we can."

"You really think we're in trouble here?"

"Humor me. Call it woman's intuition."

I heard him rustling around in his pockets.

"Until a few months ago," he said, "I used to be a heavy smoker . . ."

"Well, thanks for sharing."

"Aw! Good!"

A snap was followed by an orange glow as the match he'd just struck allowed him to look at me. And vice versa. He was smiling.

"Thought I might still have some matches on me," he said. Then his expression turned grave. "You really think we're in trouble, huh?"

"I really think we're in trouble."

" 'Cause if this is just the result of a storm, if we're just accidentally stalled here . . ."

"You mean, like Midrail #417 got 'accidentally' derailed?"

He swallowed. "You have a point, Peterson, Ow!"

The match had burned his fingertips. He dropped it. The smell of smoke curled gently up as he lit another one. He held it aloft, illuminating the ceiling of elevator car, and revealing the square outline of a service port.

"I'll give you a boost," he said. "See if you can pop that sucker open."

"Okay. . . ."

"Slip your shoes off."

I did.

He shook out the match, and said, "Feel around till you can find my hands . . . that's *not* my hands!"

"Ooops. Sorry."

Now that I'd located the stirrup he'd made of his hands, I put my right foot in his grasp and he lifted me up. I pushed the ceiling piece up and over, sliding it to one side. A glass skylight high above allowed moonlight to cascade down the elevator shaft, its metal beams looking abstract and oddly beautiful in the ivory glow.

I grabbed on to both sides of the opening and hoisted myself on top of the elevator. I was breathing hard; it was strangely exhilarating up here. So far, I was more excited than frightened.

Looking down into the elevator, where Brackett was looking up, I said, "I can try to pull you up . . ."

"No need. Move aside—I think I can use the phone box as a step."

I moved aside, heard him grunting down there—obviously, he didn't work out, which a man his age really should—and then suddenly he was lifting himself up through the portal and on top of the elevator next to me.

"You're *sure* we're in trouble?" he said, rolling his eyes at me, obviously not thrilled to be sitting on top of an elevator.

"I'm pretty sure."

We had just gotten to our feet when the electricity came back on with a *whirring* sound. The car below us was illuminated again, and the elevator jolted.

We were now standing on a moving elevator.

"I'm *very* sure!"

"We're going down!" he said.

"Is that a good idea?"

"I don't *think* so . . ."

"Should we climb back inside?" I asked, pointing down at the trapdoor. More frightened than excited now.

"I got a definite feeling we oughta get off at this stop!"

He pointed to a metal ladder inside the elevator shaft, and taking me by the waist, picked me up and practically threw me onto the thing. Then I was scaling the ladder, with Brackett right behind me, not really sure of my destination.

From below came the sound of the elevator coming to a stop again, and a shifting of gears and pulleys or whatever-the-hell pulled that thing up, and up is where it began to go again. I noted this with dismay over my shoulder, as the car was heading straight toward us.

I scrambled up the ladder, Brackett on my heels (of my feet—the spikes were in the elevator, the one currently on its way up to see us), and he was saying encouraging things like, "Hurry! Hurry the hell up!" The elevator was following us (wherever it was we were going), whining and growling like a great mechanical beast intent on catching us and crushing us to marmalade. Which may not have been its intent, actually, but would certainly be the outcome if I didn't move my well-toned behind.

Rung after rung, I scurried upward, and I saw light at the end of the tunnel, or rather the access hatch at the side of the skylight. I allowed myself a breath of relief, but that breath caught in my throat.

"Open it *now*!" Brackett called, just below me. "Damn thing's only six feet away!"

"It's stuck!"

The hatch wouldn't budge. I felt him on me, climbing around me, like my body was part of the ladder, and then he had one arm around me, holding on to a rung, and with the other hand was helping me push, push, *push*, and then the little metal door burst open.

He hiked me up and through it. I could hear the

great grinding beast of the elevator just heartbeats away. Then I was on the roof and I looked down, and there the thing was, bearing down on Brackett, or rather up. I leaned down and held out my hand and he grabbed it and I yanked him up and through and onto the roof as the elevator clanged to a stop, inches from the portal we'd escaped through.

We tumbled together onto the gravel-covered roof, winding up in the missionary position, the wind howling around us.

"Thanks, Peterson."

"Don't mention it."

He rolled off me, and we both sat there, panting, trying to get our breath back.

"That's about all the trouble I can handle for one night," he said.

The gunshot might have been thunder on this stormy night, but it wasn't. It was a gunshot all right, kicking up the nearby gravel.

"Too bad!" I said, and got to my feet, and so did Brackett, and we had to work at it to stay upright in the gusty wind. The wind turned our heads back to where the shot had come from, and there he was.

A man in a parka and fancy-design, steel-toed cowboy boots, standing on the rooftop, pointed a rifle at us, like we were antelopes he was hoping to bag across a plain.

"Shit An M-16!" Brackett said, looking around quickly, and nodding toward a roof-mounted satellite dish perhaps ten feet away. He grabbed my hand and pulled me along the graveled roof. "Keep down!"

It was advice I didn't need—I was already crouching, just like he was, doing my best against the merciless wind. The neck scarf was blowing in my face and I kept batting it away. We took cover behind the satellite dish, huddling together.

"*He's* gotta be having trouble, too!" Brackett said into my ear.

"What do you mean?"

"Getting a good shot at us in this gale."

A barrage of gunfire slammed into the dish, pounding it, shaking it on the metal pole that was its base, whining and echoing into the night.

"Yeah," I said, shivering with cold, among other things, "he *does* have it tough!"

Brackett peeked around the satellite dish. "He's reloading," he said.

Another skylight was just behind us, sloping gradually to another level of the rooftop. Beyond the skylight was a huge air-conditioning unit.

"There may be another trapdoor or something behind that," Brackett said, nodding in that direction. He slipped his arm around my waist, and we started down the pitched skylight.

We were hanging on to each other for support as we tried to walk on the metal framework of the skylight and not the glass. Then my stupid scarf blew in Brackett's face and he lost his balance momentarily, and his foot crashed through a pane of glass, shattering it.

The noise was the loudest thing I'd ever heard.

Or would be, until the next, inevitable barrage of bullets from the rifle somewhere behind us. . . .

But we made it to the air-conditioning unit without getting shot, and crouched there.

"I don't see any trapdoor," I said.

"Give me that damn thing," he said, and clawed at my scarf.

He hooked it through the louvers of the air-conditioning unit and allowed it to whip in the wind.

"Now," Brackett whispered, smiling tightly, "let's circle around, and come back the way we came."

We were climbing back down and through the access hatch on the skylight above the elevator car we'd abandoned, when we heard the thunderous gunfire on the other side of the rooftop, as my fluttering scarf attracted the assassin's latest fusillade. Most likely, he'd just killed an air-conditioning unit, dead.

Once again we were on top of the elevator, and Brackett lowered me gently through the trapdoor, and then I reached up and helped him down. We stood there for a moment, feeling safe within the elevator, and my grin must have been just as shit-eatingly self-satisfied as his. Then his eyes softened and I thought maybe he was going to . . .

But then I saw him: the cowboy assassin!

He had stuck his scowling face through that skylight access panel, wind blowing like hell all round him, and was looking down at us through the trapdoor atop our elevator car!

I pulled Brackett to one side, hit the Lobby button. We could see the cowboy with the M-16, taking aim down through the trapdoor. How I wished we'd taken the time to pull that panel back in place, but we hadn't, and now all we could do was plaster ourselves against the wall of the moving elevator, and hope he couldn't get us in his sights.

Brackett risked a peek, and said, "He's in the shaft. He's climbing onto that ladder!"

"What's he think he's *doing*?"

"I don't know, but I'm not giving him a better target."

Brackett reached out for the box by the phone and hit a switch, plunging our car back into darkness.

Maybe it startled the assassin.

Maybe he just lost his footing.

Whatever the case, just as we were nearing the bottom, a helpless scream came echoing down the shaft after us, getting closer and louder, and closer and louder, until there was a *whump* like I never heard before or since, as he landed on top of the elevator, after a fifteen or more stories drop.

We were still moving.

Brackett flicked the lights back on.

Above us the cowboy's face was looking right at us, his head hanging down through the trapdoor, his eyes wide and empty and dead.

The elevator hit bottom just hard enough to send the cowboy's body down through the trapdoor and thudding onto the floor of the car. Brackett and I, clutching each other reflexively like a couple of scared teenagers at a *Friday the 13th* movie, got out of his way.

Then there was an awkward moment as we left each other's arms, and Brackett bent down to have a closer look at the late assassin.

As he was doing that, the elevator doors opened onto an empty lobby. I hit the switch that stopped the elevator. I didn't think it should be taking any other passengers, not for a while.

Brackett was checking the man's wallet, finding a little cash, nothing much else. I spotted a slip of paper sticking half-out of the parka pocket, kneeled down, and plucked it out.

It said: "Ext. 307."

I showed it to Brackett.

"Mean anything to you?" I asked.

"No. How about you?"

"No."

We both exited the elevator, and faced each other warily and wearily.

"You know, Peterson," he said, "if *I* knew what you knew, and *you* knew what *I* knew, maybe we could get to the bottom of this, *and* live to enjoy our Pulitzers."

I thought that over.

"Then maybe we should call on Mrs. Beekman," I said, "together."

10

Bail Out

BYLINE: Peter Brackett

The kite was still in the tree, despite the wind's efforts to rattle the branches. It was silhouetted there in the moonlight, as if family life here had been abandoned in midsentence. That treacherous wind had died down some by the time we—that is, Sabrina Peterson and I—were standing on the front stoop of the Beekman house in Hinsdale.

No lights on in the place. I'd never seen a darker house.

I knocked.

"This doesn't feel right," Peterson said.

I knocked again.

Several long momemts later, Peterson reached out a hand and tried the knob. It turned. She looked at me, gave me a "why not?" shrug with expression to match, and swung the door open.

We went cautiously inside. I felt around for the light switch, found it, clicked it on. We were in a furnished living room, and yet, an empty room.

Only the large furnishings remained: sofa, easy chair, an empty bookcase. The TV was gone, and co-ax cable curled like a snake on the floor. No personal items, other than a lone, lonely boy's sneaker lying on the floor like a symbol of interrupted childhood. I walked into the next room and found a dining room table and a china cabinet, the latter emptied out.

"Somebody left in a hurry," Peterson said.

"The widow Beekman seems to have taken only what she could fit in her car, and maybe a U-Haul."

Peterson nodded, eyes narrowing. "She didn't even call to have the electricity turned off."

We checked the master bedroom: a queen-size bed wore no sheets or spread; a chest of drawers, and a bureau, had drawers that yawned emptily. Closets were filled with empty hangers.

The boy's room, decorated with Bears and Bulls posters, told the same story: a bed, no sheets, no spread, empty drawers.

But there was a stirring in the closet.

I grabbed a lamp off a nightstand, ready to pulver-ize whoever or whatever we found, and nodded to Peterson, who turned the knob and yanked open the door, stepping quickly aside.

At first the closet seemed as empty as the others, but then we heard the faint, pitiful chirping. In the corner, in a cage, was a parakeet.

I sighed, relieved. Put the lamp down.

"I'll check the basement and the rest of the house," I said.

She nodded, holding up the parakeet cage and peering at its tiny resident. "Maybe Little Dick's gonna have a roommate," she was saying to the bird.

The basement was empty but for a washer and dryer—fairly new ones, at that. But in the den, I discovered that Mrs. Beekman hadn't taken as much trouble removing her late husband's personal items as with her own. Beekman's den was cluttered with magazines—*Scientific American*, mostly—and his desktop was littered with unpaid bills. Even his wastebasket hadn't been emptied.

Like all good reporters, I know the value of trash, and I went through the basket, where I found a small padded "Registered Mail" envelope addressed to Darryl Beekman, Jr. The return address was P.O. Box 61, Spring Creek, Wisconsin. I checked inside the envelope, but it was empty, and tossed it back in the basket.

Then I noticed something written on the back of the envelope, and retrieved it. At first I thought it said "LOE," but then realized I was looking at it upside down.

307.

The same number as on the assassin's slip of paper—ext. 307! Now I was getting someplace! I just didn't know where. I stowed the empty envelope back in the circular file, sticking it under some other trash, and pressed on.

In a desk drawer, I found a box marked XMAS CARDS—last year's. The few remaining family-photo cards showed the Beekman clan in all its glory, Mom, Dad and their ten-year-old-or-so son gathered 'round a beautifully decorated tree—"Happy Holidays From Our House to Yours - The Beekman Family."

The only problem was, the Mrs. Beekman in the

picture wasn't the pale, brunette Mrs. Beekman whom I'd met on the stoop of this very house this very afternoon.

You know—the woman who sent me to that Walton Street address where an assassin in designer cowboy boots was waiting?

Now, in our new spirit of détente, I could, perhaps *should*, have shared this with Sabrina Peterson.

Instead, I pocketed one of the cards, shoved the box back into its desk drawer, and had shut it away just before she entered, saying, "Find anything?"

"Not a scrap. How about you?"

"Nothing. This . . ."

She swallowed hard; her lip was quivering.

"What?" I asked.

"This is really scary, don't you think? Eerie, the way this house has been . . . deserted . . . in such a hurry?"

"I know." I went over to her. "It's like the day after the bomb dropped."

She shuddered. "I know I shouldn't be telling you this, but . . ."

"What?"

"I think I've *had* it with this story."

"That doesn't seem *like* you."

"Hey, I'm in way over my head on this thing. . . . I don't know *how* I let you talk me into leaving the scene of that . . . whatever it was back there on Walton Street. . . ."

"An attempt on our life, is what it was."

"Yeah, well, leaving there without calling the cops."

"It was a judgment call . . ."

She made a motion with her arms like an umpire

declaring somebody out. "Well, I've *had* it. Let's get out of here."

I walked her out. We shut the door behind us and she sat on the front stoop, her expression glum. I sat beside her. The wind was rifling the leaves of the tree, gently shaking the stranded kite.

She was hanging her head. "I hope you won't think less of me . . ."

"Are you okay, Peterson?"

"I've just *had* it with leaping off elevators and dodging bullets . . ."

She was crying!

"You *are* upset," I said.

"I can't believe I'm acting like such a . . . a . . . *girl*." She said "girl" like it was the foulest obscenity in the English language. To her, maybe it was.

I gave her my handkerchief.

"I guess I'm just not cut out for this Woodward-and-Bernstein routine," she said, her chin crinkling, her lower lip trembling. "You know, I love beating you to a scoop, I truly do, but I got my whole life stretched out in front of me, and the truth of it is . . . this thing's just too damn dangerous. I'm *scared*, Brackett."

"So am I," I said. And I wasn't just trying to make her feel better. The chill in the air wasn't only the weather. "Peterson, I postponed my book tour 'cause of this story. Getting blown away wasn't exactly part of *my* agenda, either."

"*Tell* me about it."

"I'll make ya a deal."

She looked up at me, confused, sniffling into my hanky. "A deal?"

"A deal. You quit this story, and so will I."

She blew her nose. It was her hanky, now.

"You don't have to say that," she said, "just to make me feel better."

"I'm saying it to make *me* feel better—to make us *both* feel better." I shook my head, chuckled. "Hey, gotta give you credit—you were really putting the pressure on."

"Yeah," she said, and managed a laugh. "It's been fun while it lasted."

"A kid like you, just starting out, getting your pretty face plastered on trucks and buses all over town."

"Not bad, huh? Even if I did get sent off on the occasional wild goose chase."

"Sorry about that, chief."

Her smile was endearing. "It's okay. In fact, it was clever. Inventive, even. Anyone who'd fall for a trick like that *deserves* to." She dried her eyes with a corner of the hanky. "You want this back?"

"No. Anyway, I owe you a debt of thanks for something."

She cocked her head, like the RCA pup. "Really? How so?"

"You made me remember how much I love newspapering."

That made her grin. "Hey, you're a living legend. It's been an honor just being on the same playing field as you."

In the moonlight, she looked like a child; but also a woman, a very lovely young woman with brown eyes and an inviting mouth. . . .

But all I did was stick out my hand.

And she took it, shook it, and grinned again.

"You're gonna be just fine," I said.

"I know," she said. "Give me a lift to my car?"

And—after she went in to retrieve the parakeet

in its cage—I drove her in my Cadillac to her Saab, dropping her off with a wave and a smile.

Then I used my car phone to make the plane reservations to Spring Creek, Wisconsin.

11

Friendly Skies

—

BYLINE: Sabrina Peterson

The first leg of the trip to Spring Creek, Wisconsin, was first class. I usually fly coach, truth be told, but the only last-minute accommodations available were in first, and my editor, Rick Medwick, said, considering the way I was "goosing" circulation, that the *Globe* could afford springing for it, for once.

I suppose it wasn't sporting of me to withhold a lead from Peter Brackett after we'd thrown in together last night. Hadn't we survived an encounter in an elevator shaft with the Grim Reaper in cowboy boots?

But in my defense, I didn't really feel I could trust him. Which is why I hadn't told him about the newspaper I'd found lining the cage of that abandoned parakeet in the closet.

The newspaper—several pages from the *Spring Creek Clarion* of Spring Creek, Wisconsin—was not so much interesting for what was there, but for what wasn't: An article on the front page had been clipped out.

I'd made some calls and had the missing article faxed to me first thing this morning; the article's headline read: *Darryl Beekman, Sr., Pioneer in Biotechnology Retires from Chess Chemical.*

That fax was tucked in my carryon as I got onto the plane and took my first-class seat next to a man reading the *Chronicle.* At least this morning's edition didn't feature a Peter Brackett headline exclusive (neither one of us had been in a position to discuss in print our elevator adventure of the evening before).

My fellow passenger's face was covered by the paper he was reading, but his blue jeans and cowhide jacket made me think of the cowboy assassin of the night before, and I glanced at the floor.

Steel-toed, designer cowboy boots!

Shit! Was there a battalion of bumpkins out looking for me to do me in and silence the power of the press? This wasn't that cadaverous-faced creep who saw me leaving Danny Brown's apartment, was it?

Then a flight attendant came along, wondering if we'd like anything to drink before takeoff (a bewildering experience to those of us accustomed to flying coach) and the man reading the *Chronicle* lowered the paper, revealing himself to be a friendly looking fella with a goatee and a barrel chest in a plaid shirt.

The goateed passenger ordered a Bloody Mary, gave me a quick smile, and returned to his *Chronicle.*

I was just sighing in relief when Peter Brackett stepped on board.

He'd just made it. The cabin door was closing behind him and a flight attendant looked over his ticket. He stood there like a scarecrow in the aisle, swaying just a little, carryon in hand, in a yellow shirt and tan slacks, sweater over his arm, sunglasses on a face that looked both puffy and hastily shaved. He had not been up long.

I tried to sink into my seat, but then there he was, hovering over me. He looked as though if somebody breathed hard on him, he might topple onto me.

"Excuse me," he said.

"What?" I said.

"I think you're in my seat."

"Who, me?"

"No," the goateed passenger said, moving heavily in the seat beside me, "me! Sorry, friends! I'm supposed to be 'cross the aisle. Too early in the mornin' for me to be thinkin' straight."

"Tell me about it," Brackett said.

The goateed passenger gathered his things and squeezed past me, and took the seat across the way. Then Brackett edged by me and settled into the window seat. He was still wearing his sunglasses; he was in a brooding mood. Or just plain tired.

"Look, Brackett . . ."

"I don't wanna talk till I've had my morning cup of coffee."

I knew enough to leave him alone. I sipped my orange juice.

The flight attendant, whose pretty blondness attracted Brackett's attention despite the early hour, came by with a stack of newspapers.

"Morning paper, sir?" she asked him glowingly.

What was I, the Invisible Woman?

Brackett reached across, rudely, and snatched a *Chronicle* off the stack.

"Do you have a *Globe*?" I asked her.

"No shortage of those," she said, and gave me one.

"Thank you so," I said.

We sat reading, saying nothing to each other. With the sunglasses off, his face really looked puffy. Shortly after takeoff, the flight attendant was back with a tray of brimming champagne glasses.

"No thanks," I said. "Could I just have another orange juice?"

"Why of course," the flight attendant said.

Brackett reached across me again. "I'll have the champagne, thanks."

He gulped a glass, traded the attendant his empty one for another full one, then returned to his paper.

"Morning coffee, huh?" I said.

Still looking at the paper, he said, "I was just looking for a review, but I can't seem to find it."

"Of what?"

"Your performance last night."

"Oh, is *yours* in there? You gave quite a little show yourself."

He looked away from the paper and gave me a smile as sarcastic as it was wide. "Maybe, but I couldn't muster any tears. You were brilliant. Truly. Glenn Close material. A Meryl Streep moment."

I tried not to smile. "Well, thank you. I try."

He resumed his reading, or pretended to. "By the way, our friend in, or rather, *on* the elevator last night, he was a pro out of South America."

I put my paper down. "How do you know that?"

"Friends in low places." He put his paper down, too, and looked at me earnestly—or seemed to. "I told you last night, Peterson, if I tell you what I know, and you tell me what you know . . ."

"That sounds good, only it's not my job to tell you anything. You're the competition."

"True enough. But if we keep going off on our own like this, one of us is gonna end up writing the other guy's obituary."

I could have made a crack, but the look in those pale blue eyes was serious. He was not acting. This was not an Al Pacino moment: he was sincere, and deadly serious.

"What are you suggesting?"

He swallowed. It wasn't easy for him to say it. "That we team up."

"I have no desire to be your little 'Girl Friday' . . ."

"I know you don't. We'd write separately, file our own stories with our own respective papers. But we investigate together."

"No secrets?"

"None. We'd be like the Hardy Boys . . . except one of us would be a girl. Woman."

"Let's say we're like Nancy Drew and her friend Bess . . . only in this case, Bess would be a *boy*."

He grinned in a rumpled way. "I can accept that. Deal?"

"I don't mean to interrupt . . ."

It was the attractive blond flight attendant again. She was leaning in with an expression that I could only characterize as simpering, holding a copy of Brackett's hardcover novel, *White Lies*.

"Excuse me, Mr. Brackett, but I'm reading your book, and I just *love* it."

"Well, thank you."

"I can't put it down—really! Could I impose on you to autograph it for me?"

"No imposition at all."

"Just make it out to 'Heather.' "

Her name was Heather? It would be.

Brackett was saying, "You got a pen, Peterson?"

"The last time you didn't give it back," I reminded him.

"This time I will."

I dug a pen out of my purse, then had a momentary shudder as I realized it was the silver ballpoint I'd picked up off the floor in Danny Brown's apartment. The ballpoint he'd written his last message on. . . .

"Something the matter?" Brackett asked, looking at me strangely.

"No . . . not at all. Here."

As he was signing the book to her, the flight attendant said to me chirpily, "It's a wonderful read. Have *you* read it yet?"

"Me? Uh, no . . . actually, I haven't got 'round to it yet. Keep meaning to, but . . ."

I shrugged and smiled, as Brackett handed the book back to her, saying, "There you go."

"Thank you!" The flight attendant read the inscription and began to beam. "*Thank* you. Is that in the 312 area code?"

Brackett gave me a quick embarrassed look, then smiled sheepishly. "Yes, it is. I'm not there much, but the machine's always on."

She clutched the book to her bosom and went away. At least in coach, the attendants aren't so damn friendly and omnipresent.

He was watching her go, starting to tuck my pen away in his side sports coat pocket.

I cleared my throat. "I may need that. I write for a living, you know."

"Oh. Sorry."

He gave me the pen back and I slipped it in my purse, shaking my head, rolling my eyes.

"So," he said, "is it a deal?"

"Is what a deal?"

"Are we a team?"

"Well . . . I suppose it is the sensible, practical thing to do, in this case."

"Of course it is." He gave me a narrow-eyed look. "But you *do* know what it means?"

"What does it mean?"

He shrugged, raising an eyebrow. "That we have to start telling each other the truth. That we have to be completely honest with each other."

"Ah."

"No more double crosses."

"No more wild goose chases?"

"No more lies."

"No more tricks?"

"Not a one."

He raised his champagne glass, and I lifted my orange juice cup, and we toasted.

"Partners," he said.

"Partners," I said. I finished my orange juice, then said, "I shouldn't have had two glasses of this stuff. Excuse me."

I undid my seat belt and stepped out into the aisle.

It was cramped in the little restroom, but I leaned over the counter, rifling Brackett's billfold, which I'd lifted when he scooched past me taking his seat. I didn't find much of interest until I came to a folded item that proved to be the Beekman family Christmas card.

I studied it, wondering what had been so significant about this that Brackett had bothered taking it—*and* not telling me about it.

When I got back to my seat, Brackett had started in on my *Globe*.

"Your taste is improving," I noted, and sat down, and buckled up, and as I leaned forward, I noticed that my carry-on bag under the seat in front of me seemed to have shifted.

And the zipper wasn't completely zipped.

The dishonest louse had been ransacking my things!

I didn't reveal my irritation. I just leaned over, zipped it tight, and dropped his wallet on the floor near his feet.

"Is this yours?" I said, holding up the wallet as if I'd just found it.

"Uh, yeah . . ." He was thinking it over. "Thanks . . . I guess."

"You should be more careful. Look, Brackett"—I put on my sweetest, primmest smile—"since we're partners . . ."

"Yes?"

"I have something to confess. . . ."

He put his paper down, raising both eyebrows. "Please do."

"The reason I'm on my way to Wisconsin is this." I reached down and pulled my carryon out from under the seat and plopped it into my lap, unzipping it, and found the *Clarion* pages that had lined the parakeet's birdcage. I handed him the pages, and he pretended to be looking them over for the first time.

He said, "There's an article missing . . ."

"I know."

He gave me a studied look. Then he dug out his billfold and peeled out the Beekman Christmas greeting like paper money. "Take a look at this."

I pretended to look at it for the first time. "What's it mean?" I asked, handing the folded card back to him.

"You only spoke to Mrs. Beekman on the phone."

"Right. And she sent me to Walton Street, God bless her."

"Well, *I* saw her in the flesh. Remember, I told you? I went to the Beekman house yesterday afternoon, to get *my* near-fatal invite to Walton Street?"

"Right."

He flicked the Christmas card with the nail of his middle finger and it made a *click*. "This isn't the same Mrs. Beekman I saw at that house."

"What?"

"Unless Darryl Beekman, Jr., got divorced and remarried since last Christmas, the 'Mrs. Beekman' who gave us that invitation to die was *not* Mrs. Beekman at all."

"Who *was* she?"

"I don't know. A bad guy!"

Now I studied him. He was reeking sincerity and openness, damn him.

So I took a chance. "Here's the missing article," I said, and took the fax out of my slacks pocket and handed it to him.

" 'Biotechnology,' " he read. "This is Darryl Beekman, *Senior*?"

"Yes. Darryl, Jr.'s dad. I figure he's a guy worth talking to."

He was still gazing at the fax, like it was a crystal

ball he was trying to make out his future out in. "Definitely," he said. "Did you run a data-base check on him?"

"I couldn't," I said, embarrassed. "Our system's been canceled."

"Mine hasn't. I can do it from the hotel."

"We should stay at the same one."

"We are. I had my secretary do some calling around this morning."

"Is that how we wound up on the same plane?"

He shook his head "no." "I knew the airline the *Globe* has an account with. If you were on a plane to Wisconsin this morning, this had to be it. Say, *this* is odd . . ."

"What is?"

He was frowning at the faxed article. "Says here Beekman left his job at Chess Chemical after twenty-eight years."

"What's so odd about that?"

"Most of these big companies retire guys like that out at *thirty* years."

"So?"

"So why would anyone leave his job two years short of full retirement benefits?"

"Maybe it's just an early retirement, with full benies. A lot of companies these days . . ."

He shook his head "no" again. "Not a top research guy like this. If anything, they find a way to hang on to a brain like this longer. So why'd he retire early?"

"How should I know? I've only been Nancy Drew for fifteen minutes."

His smile was one-sided, but this time it didn't seem so smug.

"Hey, *I* figured it out," he said, "and how long have I been Bess?"

12

Cash Cow

BYLINE: Peter Brackett

A herd of holsteins were grazing in pastoral splendor, blissfully ignorant of encroaching civilization as represented by the cheerful billboard that said, WELCOME TO SPRING CREEK, WISCONSIN— HOME OF CHESS CHEMICAL. Smaller letters added this Orwellian coda: *Striving for a Better Tomorrow, Today.*

We glided in Sabrina Peterson's rental Mustang convertible (thank you, Chicago *Globe*) through the small one-company town, taking in its well-manicured lawns and Victorian homes along the well-shaded thoroughfare that led us back out into the country.

Which was where we were headed: to the country lane where Dr. Darryl Beekman, Sr., resided.

"Here!" she said.

I turned onto the gravel road.

"Slow down! That last number was twenty-four, so the Beekman place has got to be next."

I slowed down. Half a mile or so later, a mailbox said "Beekman" and I swung into the adjacent narrow lane.

My jaw dropped; so did Peterson's. We exchanged wide-eyed looks and then returned our gaze to the cause of those dropped jaws and wide-eyed looks: a scorched patch of ground with the charred remnants of what had been, before the conflagration, a house.

The Beekman house.

I stopped, got out, and so did Peterson. We wanted a closer look, not believing our eyes. We couldn't get much closer without stepping over the yellow fire department tape. And we didn't bother doing that, because there was nothing to see.

Just scorched earth.

Somewhere, in the nearby distance, a cow mooed. It was as unsettling as the cry of hyena.

We were hunkered down over the microfilm machine in the stately, turn-of-the-century brick edifice housing the Spring Creek library.

I read aloud: " 'Dr. Darryl M. Beekman, Sr., genetic engineering pioneer at Chess Chemical died Tuesday in a fire in his Spring Creek home. . . .' "

"What's the date on that obit?" Peterson asked, practically sticking her head in my field of vision.

"Exactly one week before the Midrail crash."

"The plot sickens," she said, and then she read aloud: " 'Dr. Beekman's house was completely destroyed in the blaze. Identification was established through dental records.' "

"You're crowding me, Peterson!"

"All right, then," she said. "*You* read it first, then I will."

She stood and paced nearby, nervously. I couldn't blame her. The scent of death—more specifically, murder—was hanging over this story like the burnt stench at what had been the Beekman place.

I read to myself:

> While at Chess Chemical, Dr. Beekman served as head researcher on the Livestock Development Factor (LDF), a genetically engineered hormone for dairy cows.

I jotted down the initials "LDF" on my notepad, and suddenly Peterson was hovering over me like a teacher who thought I was cheating.

"What's *that*?"

She seemed almost startled.

"What's what?"

She put her finger on the letters "LDF." "*That.*"

I shrugged. "It's some genetically engineered hormone to make cows give more milk. It's been in the news. Like those biotech tomatoes. Don't you read the papers?"

But she didn't say anything. Her eyes were glazed, her complexion as pale as milk—but looking not nearly as healthy.

What did she know that I didn't?

I pushed my chair back with a screech, which got a "*Shush!*" from a passing, matronly librarian, and said, "That's it."

"What?"

I threw up my hands. "I've had it."

She frowned, then leaned in to have a look at the microfilm screen while I gathered my notebook and walked quickly out of there, footsteps echoing.

Outside, under a blue sky on as nice a sunny day as God ever put together, I scowled and opened the trunk of the Mustang and yanked out my carry-on bag. A gigantic girl of maybe eight, wearing a baseball cap sideways, sporting a big smile and a milk mustache, was saluting me with her glass of healthy white liquid from a "Wisconsin Dairy Farmers" billboard across the street.

"Retaining water, are we?" Peterson's voice said.

I turned to her. "I should've known you were trouble the minute I saw you. I should've known to steer you a wide path."

She winced in confusion and irritation. "What are you *talking* about?"

"I'm dissolving our partnership."

"What! What for?"

I waggled a scolding finger at her. "Because you lied to me. I saw the look on your face when you saw those initials."

"Initials?"

"LDF! You won't tell me what you know, well, that's just peachy. It's every girl for herself from here on out." I tossed her the car keys and she caught them, but blinked in surprise.

"You're on your own," I told her.

Her big brown eyes became slits in her face; she put her hands on her hips and leaned forward accusingly. "Are you saying you haven't held *anything* back from *me*?"

"Nothing!"

"Is that right? Well, you never mentioned one

little item. How did you *know* I'd be flying to Wisconsin this morning?"

"I told you, I had my secretary check—"

"On flights to Wisconsin. Why *Wisconsin*, Brackett?"

"Well, I . . . I sort of found an envelope addressed to Darryl, Jr., with a Spring Creek return address."

"You sort of found it. Where, at Darryl, Jr.'s place in Hinsdale? What, in the wastebasket?"

I swallowed. "Yeah. It had extension 307 written on it, too."

Her eyes widened; fear was back. "Like the number on that slip of paper in the cowboy's parka pocket?"

I nodded.

She walked over and sat on the cement steps of the ancient library. She looked dazed. Idly, she said, "Took you long enough to level about that *Christmas* card, too. . . ."

I sat next to her. "What do you mean?"

She gave me a toss of her hair. "I saw it in your billfold."

"I *thought* you picked my pocket! Jesus, Peterson—you're incorrigible!"

She smirked glumly, leaning her elbow on her knee, propping her chin up with her fist. "Then don't 'incorrige' me."

"I would've told you about that address, *and* that number. . . ."

"When? When you finally got me in the sack?"

I frowned. "What are you talking about?"

She laughed with a snort, and shook her head. "I know all about your reputation. Nobody 'scores' with the 'ladies' as often as Peter 'little-white-lies' Brackett. Well, I got news for ya, buddy boy—you're *not* my *type*."

"Not *your* type. You're not *my* type!"

"Well . . ." She looked like she was going to bicker some more, but then it went away. "Maybe that's just as well. Maybe we can keep this strictly business."

"You mean—resume our partnership?"

She nodded. Lord, she was pretty.

"Okay," I said. "I should've told you about the Christmas card earlier, and I should've told about the envelope with extension 307 on it, too."

"Is that an apology?"

"No. It's a preamble to me asking you what the hell you know about LDF."

Her expression changed; she began to tremble.

"Are you *acting* again?"

She shook her head "no," almost violently, then sat with her hands folded, her shoulders all pulled in, as though she were trying to disappear.

"I saw those letters . . . or at least the first two of them . . . written on a dead boy's hand."

And she told me—finally, haltingly—about Danny Brown.

I arched an eyebrow. "I guess last night *wasn't* the first time you left a crime scene without calling the cops."

"No. I'm way in over my head, aren't I?"

"That guy you hear gurgling next to you is me. Let's go."

"Where?"

"Back inside. Let's see what else that microfilm machine has to say. . . ."

*   *   *

What it had to say was that Chess Chemical was now considered to be at the "forefront of biotechnology" thanks to LDF, which would soon "transform the barnyard." Into what, it didn't say. It did say that the projected "commercial success" of the genetically engineered hormone would be a breakthrough in "the new age of edible biotechnology."

"And I thought 'New Age' was just bad music and funky crystals," I said.

"This is big," said Peterson.

We were huddled, cozily this time, around the microfilm machine.

"Somebody tried to kill us over a *cow* hormone?" I asked. "Are you kidding?"

"Somebody isn't," she said, and pointed to another headline: CHESS ANNOUNCES GLOBAL PLANS FOR LDF.

"Global plans," I said. "In other words, big bucks."

"As in billions," she said.

"Hey, wait—here it says 'critics fear the hormone will cause certain health problems in cows, requiring antibiotics which could show up as residue in the milk supply.' The FDA is expected to gave it the green light, but the state legislature is reviewing the LDF milk test themselves."

She was nodding as she read. "It says the agriculture committee is headed up by Gayle Robbins." She gave me a sharp glance. "I've heard of her—they say she's going to run for the U.S. Senate next year. . . ."

"I've heard of her, too," I said, and smiled.

"Don't hold out on me!"

"Oh, I'm not. Got your map? We're goin' to the state capital, Madison."

13

Cows at the Capitol

—

BYLINE: Sabrina Peterson

The capitol in downtown Madison was typically stately, but surprisingly close to the nearby storefronts as it sat in the midst of the square, although what was perhaps more surprising were the cows grazing on the capitol lawn. Brackett and I traded astonished, amused looks as we walked from the parking ramp where we left the Mustang, noting the clean-cut-looking farm kids, who were tending to these heifers munching lackadaisically at the grass. A golden, Grecian-type woman in a flowing robe oversaw her bovine subjects dispassionately from atop the domed capitol.

"They call it 'Cows on the Concourse,'" Sam Smotherman explained, as he walked us along a busy capitol corridor. A small, affable, self-confident man, Smotherman held a stack of folders in one hand and an unlighted cigar in the other. He and Brackett were old friends.

" 'Cows on the Concourse?' " Brackett said.

"It's a yearly way of honoring the state's most important citizens: the dairy farmers. You know, celebrating the contribution of cows to our culture."

"Oh, brother," Brackett said.

"Of course, last year the hog farmers wanted equal time."

"Don't tell me," Brackett said.

"That's right." Smotherman grinned. " 'Pigs on the Concourse'! Stay tuned for chickens. . . ."

"What can you tell us about LDF?" I asked. "We understand your boss, Senator Robbins, is looking into it."

"Her committee is, yes." He was hustling along and we had to work to keep up. "Hope you don't mind if we walk and talk . . . but this has been one crazy day."

"Not at all," Brackett said.

"Mr. Speaker," Smotherman said, nodding to a distinguished-looking older gentleman going in the opposite direction, then said to us, "If you want to know about LDF, you came to the right place. Shoot."

That was an expression I wasn't wild about after last night's skirmish in the elevator shaft.

"What is LDF, exactly?" Brackett asked. "In layman's terms."

"In layman's terms, it's a time-saver . . . and potential money-maker. Usually takes a calf two years to mature into a milk-producing cow. Chess Chemical figured why wait that long, caring for a cow that isn't making you any dough, when you can speed things up a little?"

"So they invented LDF?" I offered.

"Correct," Smotherman said. "They can shoot this hormone into newborn calves and in nine months, bingo: ya got yourself a full-grown, milk-producing, money-making heifer."

"Ready to graze on the concourse," Brackett said wryly.

"You got it."

"Sounds like Franken-milk to me" I said, shivering.

"That's an understandable reaction," Smotherman said, "but kinda knee-jerk, don't you think? Chess says LDF milk is one-hundred-percent safe and, from what we hear, their tests bear 'em out. . . . excuse me."

He stopped a young woman and asked her a question about some notes for a pending bill, and she patiently told him they were in his folder. He rolled his eyes, checked one of his folders, laughed, and moved on. We stayed with him.

"What's the profit potential of this thing?" Brackett asked.

"Once their test results are approved by the FDA, they stand to make something like . . . what was it I read? A billion? A billion and a half a year?"

"Give or take half a billion," I said.

Brackett gave a low whistle.

"Yeah, it's major, all right," Smotherman said. "Probably revolutionize the dairy industry. So—what's the deal? Why are Chicago's two star reporters interested in a dairy hormone?"

"Peterson here is a big milk drinker," Brackett said.

"I can see that," Smotherman said. "Does a body good."

I smiled, as if this sexist twaddle had struck me as complimentary.

"Okay, then," Smotherman said, smiling sideways at us, "don't level with me. But if the *Chronicle* and the *Globe* are in bed together, it's gotta be big."

"We're not exactly in *bed* together," I said.

Smotherman looked at Brackett and gave him a fake sad look. "Pity," he said, and laughed.

What a jerk.

We had rounded a corner, now, stopping at a door labeled CONFERENCE ROOM. A petite, dark-haired, forty-something woman, trim and attractive in a gray business suit, approached Smotherman with a pleasant but pointed look.

"Are you ready?" she asked.

"Always," Smotherman said. "But take two seconds and say hello to some friends from Chicago. Senator Gayle Robbins, Sabrina Peterson from the *Globe*, and Peter Brackett from the *Chronicle*."

"Pleasure," she said, and we shook hands all around. Then she asked, "What brings you to Madison?"

"They're researching a story on LDF," Smotherman said.

"Really?" She smiled, but there was an intensity behind her eyes. "And what's your take on this wonder hormone?"

"We wonder what your *take* is," I said.

The senator smirked. "Off the record?"

"Sure," I said, and Brackett nodded.

"Off the record, I'd file it under 'who needs it?' I mean, messing around with milk . . . it even *sounds* un-American."

"Off the record," Brackett said, "why do you want your opinion 'off the record?' "

Smotherman answered for her. "Because it's not prudent for us to offer an opinion on LDF before the FDA makes its decision."

"On the *other* hand . . ." the senator began, but an assistant poked his head out of the conference room and interrupted her with a question.

"If you'll excuse me," the senator said.

But I pressed. "You started to say, 'on the other hand.' "

"Oh. Well, it just seems to me that the only people who stand to benefit from LDF are named Chess."

"Chess?"

"The Chess family, who own Chess Chemical."

Brackett said, "What about the farmers, who save all that time and money with these super-heifers?"

"That's what investigations and hearings are all about, Mr. Brackett. And that's why we're off the record—I really don't know enough about this subject yet, to speak intelligently about it. But if you come up with something interesting where LDF is concerned, you will let me know?"

"It's a promise," Brackett said.

Then she disappeared into the conference room. Smotherman was about to go in, too, but he stopped and put a hand on Brackett's shoulder.

"I know, I know—you two still have a couple thousand questions. I'll be done in about an hour. How about I take you two out for a nice, big, juicy Wisconsin-bred steak?"

"Sure," Brackett said, "if you'll hold the LDF."

* * *

"Two New York strips, medium rare," our waiter said, as he delivered our three dinners, "and one steamed vegetables, no butter, no oil."

The steak house in downtown Madison, a stone's throw from the capitol, was your typical red carpet, dark-wood affair and we were ensconced in a comfy booth in back. My two male dinner companions were staring in horror over their slabs of bloody beef at me and my vegetable plate, as if *I* were the one eating a dead animal.

"You were saying?" I prompted Smotherman.

"What? Oh." He blinked a couple times. "Chess Chemical." He shrugged, picked up a steak knife and cut into the black slab in front of him, revealing bright red. "You know how they made their mark, in the sixties, don't you?"

"Napalm, Agent Orange, and other goodies," Brackett said, cutting his own steak open, as if exposing a bloody wound. I could barely eat my vegetables, watching them.

"But when the Vietnam war ended," Smotherman said, "profits started drying up . . . until the eighties rolled around, and the genetic revolution gave 'em a shot in the arm."

"What about the Chess family?" I asked. "What are they like?"

Smotherman shrugged. "The old man's a zealot of sorts . . . he's run for governor a couple times."

"Sounds like he wants to be Ross Perot when he grows up," Brackett said, chewing.

"He's more right wing than populist," Smotherman said. "Anyway, he's busy dabbling in matters political. The business is pretty much left to his son now. Wilson. Willy, his friends call him. Enemies, too."

I swallowed some cauliflower. For a steak house, they didn't do veggies half bad. Nice and crisp. "You sound like you know something about him," I said.

"Not really all that much," Smotherman said. He ate a bite of baked potato, with sour cream and butter; a true cholesterol time bomb. "Went straight from Yale to Daddy's corporate team."

Smotherman stopped a passing waiter to ask for some A-1 Sauce.

"Did you know Willy at Yale?" Brackett asked.

"No—I think he's a little younger than me. We probably weren't there quite at the same time. That's some memory you got there, Pete—ever think about going into journalism?"

"I'm trying to discourage him," I said.

"You know," Smotherman was saying thoughtfully, a speared chunk of rare beef on his fork poised for oblivion, "I'm not sure Willy even graduated. There have always been a few grumblings about the guy."

"Such as?" I asked.

"Just that he's the kind of a fella who gets to run a big company only one way in hell: if his daddy owns the sucker."

"That's the American way," Brackett said wryly.

"If he had graduated," I asked, "what year would that have been?"

"Oh, God, I don't know," Smotherman said, then thought. "Let's see, I graduated in '73 . . . no, '74. So he'd probably be class of '76 or maybe '77."

I jotted that down in my notebook.

Smotherman gestured with a hand holding a well-buttered piece of roll. "You know, Gayle—Senator Robbins—has met with Willy a few times. He's got an office at Chess Chemical on the top floor of what they affectionately call the 'Black Tower.' "

"Sounds cozy," I said.

Smotherman shook his head, cut deeper into his rapidly disappearing beef. "Chess's a pretty wacky place, at that. They're into all sorts of biotech bull-shit. Actually, LDF is a pretty tame project, for them."

"What do you mean?" Brackett asked.

"There's a thing in here," he said, and he patted the stack of files on the seat next to him, "about how they're cross-splicing genes to come up with various new species of animals."

I was *really* glad I was eating veggies now.

"Welcome to the wonderful world of tomorrow, kids," Smotherman said, and bring his napkin up off his lap to his mouth. "Anybody for dessert?"

We paused in front of the steak house. It was a clear, cool evening, and in the background the faint sound of grazing cows on the concourse provided mood music—emphasis on the *moo*.

"Here," Smotherman said, handing me his card, "in case you have any more questions. My direct line."

"Thanks," I said, tucking it away in my purse. Frankly, I wasn't terribly enamored of this glad-handing chauvinist, and wondered why an enlight-ened woman like Gayle Robbins would have anything to do with him.

On the flipside, he did seem to know his stuff.

"Where are you parked?" he asked.

"The ramp around the corner," Brackett said.

"Good!" Smotherman said, slipping between us, taking us each by the arm as we started across the street with the green light. "I'll walk along with you. . . . I may make you change your mind about dessert, yet."

"Yeah?" I said.

Smotherman smiled slyly. "We're gonna walk right past the best damn frozen yogurt joint on the face of the planet. Man, is that stuff good . . ."

The sound of squealing tires and a big engine accelerating alerted us, and we were caught in the middle of the intersection as the speeding car—I never got a good look at it, just sensed that it was big and dark and new-looking—bore right down on us, its lights like awful staring eyes.

"Christ!" Brackett said.

Smotherman stood there as frozen as his beloved yogurt, paralyzed with fear.

I dove for the sidewalk, and saw Brackett barely yank Smotherman out of the way, and onto the hood of a parked Buick. The car cut so close, it scraped against the vehicles parked along the curb, making an ungodly metallic screech, shooting crackling sparks into the night.

One split second later, and the two of them would have been just two more slabs of rare beef on the hoof.

Then the killer car skidded around the corner, and was gone.

My heart was in my throat.

Smotherman, clutching his chest, seemed to be trying to keep his heart where it was. His eyes were round and wild. "What the hell was *that* all about?"

Even Brackett was breathing hard. "No big deal," he said, getting to his feet, brushing off his slacks. "This kind of thing happens to Nancy Drew and Bess all the time."

14

Nickel Tour

BYLINE: Peter Brackett

I sat sipping coffee, nibbling a cheese Danish at a table on the patio of the Mill Creek Inn's restaurant, enjoying the peaceful view of the small, idyllic lake the quaintly countrified hotel nestled along. The morning was pleasant and cool, though according to the local paper—the Spring Creek *Clarion*—things might heat up later on.

I checked my watch: almost nine-thirty, and no sign of Peterson. Her dedication to digging out scoops apparently didn't preclude sleeping in. The early bird she was not.

On the other hand, I'd been out looking for worms for a couple of hours. Wandering the town square, I happened by a barber shop just as it was opening, and stopped in for a shave. Mr. Lee (the barber) was a fountain of knowledge where Spring Creek and its key industry were concerned. And he gave me a close shave, for a third of what it would have cost me back home.

You'd think I'd already had enough close shaves lately to hold me awhile, wouldn't you?

At quarter to ten, Peterson drifted onto the restaurant patio, looking fresh and well-scrubbed and well-rested, in a creamy jacket, dark blouse, and slacks.

I started to rise and she said, "Don't get up," sitting opposite me, gazing with a dreamy smile out at the lake where the morning sun cast a shimmering reflection.

"Want some coffee?" I asked. I'd had the waiter leave a pot.

"No thanks," she said. "I've had my herbal tea for the morning. I've been up awhile."

"Really?"

"Yes, I checked down here for you, didn't see you, then figured I shouldn't disturb you. Man your age needs his rest."

I smiled a little. "I like to think of it as a beauty sleep. Learn anything about Spring Creek while you were out strolling?"

"Who said I went out strolling?"

"I don't know." I poured myself some more coffee. "Just a hunch."

She called a waitress over and got some water. Then she said, "I did take a walk, and I sort of ended up at city hall."

"No. Really?"

She leaned across the table with a conspiratorial

gleam in her big brown eyes. "Know how that fire started?"

"Tell me."

"The file clerk in the arson records department—cute young guy named Tony—let me have a peek at the Beekman file." She flicked her nail at the coffee-pot, making a *ding*. "The fire started with a short in a coffeemaker."

"I suppose that's possible."

"Possible," she said, nodding. "But then I sort of wandered over to the local tea-and-coffee shop, and while I was buying myself some decaffinated herbal, I struck up a conversation with the sales clerk, Steve."

"Oh, you did? You met both Tony *and* Steve this morning. Friendly little town."

"Very. And Steve said that Darryl Beekman, Sr., was a regular customer. Ordered the same brand of tea for the last fifteen years."

"Tea?"

"Tea. Beekman was *not* a coffee drinker. According to Steve—and he should know—Darryl Beekman was the last person on earth who'd own a coffee-maker. . . . Have *you* been up long?"

She had leveled with me; so I leveled with her.

"I went out around eight and got a shave," I said. "The local barber told me all about this construction project his son, a carpenter, is working on. It's a big crew, lot of people brought in from out of town."

"Oh?"

"New twenty-five-million-dollar LDF facility they're putting up out at Chess Chemical."

Her expression turned astounded. "Chess is putting up a twenty-five-million-dollar facility for a product that hasn't even been *approved* yet?"

I gave her a wide-eyed nod, and sipped my coffee.

"This is incredible!" She was beaming now. "That's our story!"

"It is?"

"Oh, come on. Think about it." She moved to the seat next to mine and leaned in so close our foreheads were almost touching. "The head researcher on LDF retires early, then dies in a fire resulting from a short in a coffeemaker he never owned. A week later, his son boards a train with something important on his person, probably that briefcase I saw Danny Brown and his friends steal from the crash site. But I'm getting ahead of myself. . . . Anyway, the train crashes, the son dies. The looter who took the briefcase winds up murdered, but not before he writes the letters 'LD' on his palm for a certain reporter to see. We start unraveling the case, connecting the death of Beekman, Jr., to Beekman, Sr., and somebody tries to kill us."

"Twice," I said.

She leaned away, gesturing with both hands above her head. "It's so damn obvious! Beekman blew the whistle on LDF. The miracle hormone's a bust, and Chess Chemical has too much wrapped up in it to let the news get out!"

"Would a chemical company like Chess knowingly market a dangerous product?"

"Brackett, are you kidding? These are the same wonderful people who brought you Agent Orange and napalm, for God's sake!"

I lifted an eyebrow, and sighed. "You may have something there. There's only one thing to do."

"What?"

"Find a Ouija board and get Alfred Hitchcock's opinion."

She let out a big frustrated groan, and said, "I lay the whole story out for you, and you dismiss it with a wisecrack!"

"We could see what Oliver Stone thinks."

"Brackett!"

"I'm not dismissing you, or your opinions. I'm trying, in my feeble way, to point out to you that you *are* dealing in opinion, not fact."

I signed my room number to the check, left a dollar and some coins as a tip, and she followed me inside through the restaurant and into the rustic lobby.

"We have all *sorts* of facts!" she was protesting.

"Not enough of them."

"But we *know* that—"

I turned to her. "You can't print what you 'know,' Peterson—only what you can substantiate."

She was waving her arms. "Well, hell—let's substantiate it then! We'll go out to Chess Chemical, talk to Willy Chess, and . . ."

I lifted a cautionary finger. "Rule number one of investigative reporting, Peterson—avoid premature contact with your adversary."

Her eyes and nostrils flared. "Oh, now you're giving me the rules of investigative reporting, is that it?"

I shrugged. "Just trying to be helpful."

"You're giving rules to the reporter who out-scooped you five times in the last . . ."

"Beginner's luck."

I went out into the parking lot and she followed, fuming.

"Well, then," she said, "let me have 'em. Let's move on to rule number two!"

Over my shoulder, I said, "Rule number two is, find out what you're up against."

"How would you suggest we do that?"

I stopped at the rental Mustang, leaned against the hood, removed the folded manila envelope from my sports jacket pocket. "Take a look at this."

She removed the twenty-five-page report that Evans had faxed to me.

"Almost every line is blacked out," Peterson said, frantically scanning the sheets. "What *is* this?"

"I put in a Freedom of Information Act request on LDF."

"How did you manage this so fast . . . ?"

"The *Chronicle* has a Washington correspondent, who can make things happen, now. Someday maybe *you'll* work for a real newspaper, too, Peterson."

"Maybe *some* day," she said sarcastically. "But you pulling strings or greasing wheels or whatever-the-hell it took to get *this*"—she fluttered the report in the air accusingly at me—"didn't get us far, did it?"

"That report tells us a lot," I said. "What makes information on a cow hormone classified material? It's not exactly a list of our foreign agents and their code names."

Now she was confused. "What *would* make it classified?"

"If certain people in the government—the federal government—were clamping the lid on. If people, certain people in the FDA for example, had been bought off."

We just look at each other. All bickering ceased.

Quietly she said, "No wonder they're trying to kill us."

I pointed to the report in her hand. "*That* is what we're up against."

A trace of sarcasm edged back into her tone. "So what do you suggest, Backett? Rule number three?"

I nodded. "Exactly. Rule number three—never go in the window if the front door is open."

The towering black obelisk that was Chess Chemical's central headquarters rose from the pastoral landscape into a picture-perfect sky like a shining modernistic totem signifying a disquieting future. Around it were clustered the perfectly formed field rows and anonymous sleek sheds of research farms.

We left the Mustang in a vast parking lot, from which we were able to get a view of the partially contructed Life Sciences Building—i.e., the LDF building—where construction workers were busy, a huge crane lifting bulky steel beams. We wandered into the coldly modern, polished-marble main lobby, checking in at the massive black granite reception desk. The receptionist had a pleasant demeanor at odds with her austere surroundings, which included armed security guards in nifty uniforms that would have made the Gestapo proud.

She told us the next tour—they did a brisk tourist business—would begin in five minutes.

We sank into the cream-color leather seats of the reception area sofa.

"I thought sure extension 307 would've been a number here," she said softly.

"Me, too."

I had called Chess Chemical from the hotel, asking for extension 307, getting cafeteria services. I had spoken to Sadie, who seemed more the hair-net/

orthopedic-shoes type than a criminal mastermind trying to kill us.

I folded my arms, settled back, and then noticed that Peterson was taking notes.

"What the hell are you doing?" I whispered.

"Writing a description of this lobby," she whispered back. "Might come in handy for the story."

"Must you be so conspicuous?"

She thought about that, and was putting her spiral pad and pen back into purse, when the slip of paper with "#307" on it slipped out and onto the floor. A small pale, blandly handsome man in his late thirties or early forties—obviously an executive—was walking by, and knelt down to hand the little piece of paper back to her. His smile tried for gracious, but it was a little too practiced for my taste.

"Thank you," she said to him.

"My pleasure." He continued to smile, though his eyes were tight. "Welcome to Chess Chemical. I'm Wilson Chess."

He offered his hand. Peterson stood and shook it; her smile could have *used* some practice.

"Sabrina Peterson," she said.

Why had she given him her name? What a stupid . . .

He turned to me. "No introductions needed, here. You're Peter Brackett."

Now I was glad she had given him her real name. If he knew who I was, chances were he knew Peterson as well. I got to my feet and shook the hand he'd thrust out.

"Pleasure, Mr. Chess," I said.

"What a coincidence."

"Coincidence?"

"I'm just reading your book. *White Lies*?"

As if I needed reminding of the title.

"I hope you're enjoying it," I said.

"So far I am. Just bought it, actually. Heard such terrific things about it."

"Well, thanks very much."

"Please, please—sit back down."

We did and he sat, too, perched on the edge of the glass coffee table before us like a gnome.

"What brings you to Chess?" he asked. "Researching a story?"

"You hit it on the nose, Mr. Chess," I said. "I'm just starting a new book."

"Really? With a chemical company backdrop?"

"That's why we're here for the tour," I said. "It's a murder mystery. Lots of corporate intrigue, dirty tricks, industrial espionage, that sort of thing."

"Sounds like a winner to me. I can promise you at least one reader—I'm a real sucker for a good thriller." He turned the automatic smile back on Peterson. "What's your role in this, Ms. Peterson?"

"I'm his collaborator."

I tried not to wince.

Chess said, "Adding a woman's point of view?"

Her smile was almost a smirk. "Peter's too cynical, sometimes. My job's to make sure the bad guy gets his."

Chess thought about that a moment, then laughed. It was as forced as his smile. "I'm afraid Mr. Brackett's cynicism is well placed, Ms. Peterson. Happy endings aren't really all that realistic, in these sorry times of ours."

"I'm not looking for a happy ending," she said, "as long as justice is done."

He thought about that for a moment, too, then stood, slapped his thighs and said cheerily, "Well, it's been a treat meeting you both." He glanced behind him. "I think your tour's about to start—I'd show you around myself, but these guides of ours know a hell of a lot more about this operation that *I* do."

"Nice meeting you, Mr. Chess," Peterson said.

"Same here," I said.

He started off, then turned and said, "Don't forget to change the names to protect the innocent!"

"That's the Jack Webb way," I said pleasantly, and waved.

Peterson gave me a one-sided smile. "So much for rule number one."

I was watching Chess climb a circular marble staircase, where he paused to talk briefly to a female lab assistant. She tore the top sheet off a clipboard, handed it to him, and he went on up.

Then we were on the tour, mingling with tourists and following the lead of a chipper young woman in a Chess Chemical blazer ("Even my uniform is made of Polyvon Plus, a synthetic fiber created by our scientists here at Chess"). We learned that the carpet was stain resistant, the window glass shatterproof, all thanks to the "miracle workers in our Chess Chemical laboratories."

"Even the antihistamine I took for my hay fever this morning is a Chess product," the tour guide said in a tone that managed to be both cheerful and reverent, "and so was the sugar substitute I sprinkled on my cereal this morning."

And why not? Artificial sweetness was her specialty.

But things got a little strained when a kid of eleven or so—a boy with a baseball cap who, like the girl on the milk billboard yesterday—wandered into an alcove by a doorway marked ominously, in bold red letters: LDF RESEARCH FARM - SECURITY CLEARANCE REQUIRED. I watched with interest and a little amusement as the kid's hand touched the door and set off a blaring siren and red lights started flashing.

Half a dozen armed Chess Company security guards materialized and swarmed the kid, frightening him and his parents.

"There's nothing to be alarmed about!" the tour guide said, though I had to wonder if there was nothing to be alarmed about, why an alarm that would've woken the dead had just gone off.

The guide was working her way through the pack of armed guards, and with one hand inserted an I.D. pass in the door, disengaging the alarm, and with the other patted the eleven-year-old on the head. He was doing his best not to cry—if he'd been about a year younger, he would have.

"Sorry about the disturbance, folks!" she called out sunnily. "But we wouldn't want our competitors getting a peek at our patents!"

She guided the child—an unlikely agent of industrial espionage—back to his disturbed parents. Chess Chemical had not made friends of this family, despite all the feigned good will.

"Now," the tour guide said, leading us away from the research farm entry, "if you'll just file into the Chess IMAX Surround Sound Theater, we have a short, very informative, very entertaining film—and don't worry, Dad and Mom . . . it's rated 'G'."

"For 'give me a break,'" Peterson whispered to me.

As the tourists filed into the theater, I noticed three women in lab coats passing by.

"The blonde with glasses," I whispered to Peterson, "is the one Willy was talking to on the stairs."

Peterson and I watched as the woman went up to the LDF Research Farm door—the one that had set off the fireworks—and inserted her I.D. badge. But before she went in, one of the other two women, poised by the ladies' room doorway across the hall, called out to her.

"Kim!" the woman said, a slender redhead. "Wanna grab a smoke with us?"

Any day now, Chess Chemical would no doubt be coming up with cancer-free cigarettes. If they were testing those here, I was ready to sign up as a lab animal.

Blond, bespectacled Kim said, "Sure!", and withdrew her I.D. card and headed across the hall.

I turned my attention to the crowd filing into the theater, then glanced back to Peterson to suggest we skip the presentation.

But Peterson was gone.

15

Girl Talk

—

BYLINE: Sabrina Peterson

From the bathroom stall I could hear them chattering, and through the crack of the door, I could watch as they stood around smoking in their white lab coats. One of them, a brunette, was cute but kind of heavy, and she didn't smoke at all. She just stood primping at the mirror. The subject, of course, was men.

"I bet 'on the side' isn't the only way he had her," the pretty, dark-haired, bespectacled one said with a smirk.

"Going to Ruby's tonight, Kim?" the lanky red-head asked.

"What's the point?" Kim said, stubbing out her cigarette in an ashtray by the sink, joining the brunette in the primping ceremony. Then she sighed. "But, yeah, I'll be there."

"Want a ride?" the brunette asked. "We could all go together. Better for the environment."

They all laughed. The thought of bettering the environment was a hoot for these Chess Chemical workers.

"Naw," Kim said. "Rather have my own car, in case one of us gets lucky."

"You mean, like wins the lottery?" the redhead said wryly, and that made them laugh, too, but somewhat bitterly. Must be a shortage of single men in Spring Creek.

The ladies' room door opened and from my stall I waited until the new arrival moved into my line of vision: It was the terminally cheerful tour guide.

"I *hate* tourist season!" she said.

"Better get used to it," Kim said. "It really picks up around the holidays, you know . . ."

"I swear, if they don't get another girl to help me out, I'm quittin' this gig."

"Sure you are," the redhead said archly. "You'll love the benefits at the Gap at the Madison mall."

"Isn't that where you *used* to work?" the sweet tour guide asked, frowning at herself in the mirror, touching up her lipstick.

I waited for them to go, fixed my own makeup a little, and went looking for Brackett.

That evening I stepped out of my own room, went a few paces down the hall, and knocked on Brackett's hotel room door. Our rooms at the Mill Creek Inn were side-by-side, separated by a common door, but I didn't think I should knock on that and enter that way—didn't want to start a precedent.

I was, frankly, feeling somewhat attracted to the big jerk (I was reading and enjoying his novel, but I'd be damned if I'd admit it to him), and I wanted to try to keep things businesslike. Since our current plan of action would seem to call for me wearing my sexiest outfit—a black mini that I was poured into at the moment—keeping our "strictly business" approach in mind seemed crucial.

When the door opened, he was on the phone, stretching the cord to make the reach; his pale blue sports shirt was only half-buttoned and not tucked in. He gave me a little nod, his expression noncommittal, but his eyes said how spectacular he thought I looked.

As I came in, shutting the door behind me, he was saying into the phone, "Okay, Evans. Stay on it. I'll check with you later."

He hung up, finished buttoning his shirt, grinning like the cat that ate the canary. "I got some *really* good stuff."

I was glancing at a note he'd jotted down on a manila envelope next to the phone on his nightstand. It said: "Ernesto Vargas."

"Who's Ernesto Vargas?"

"Not the pinup artist," he said with a grin.

"Huh?" I said. I didn't follow the reference, if it was a reference to something. Like most aging baby boomers, the guy was full of obscure, pop culture allusions.

He was tucking his shirt in. "Ernesto Vargas was a pal of Willy's back at Yale."

"So Sam was right—Willy *did* go to Yale."

He sat on the edge of the bed and slipped on his shoes. They were tan leather loafers that looked like a week's pay. At the *Globe's* rates, anyway.

"Remember Sam saying he wasn't sure if Willy graduated or not?" he asked brightly. "Well, Willy not only didn't graduate, he got expelled."

"Expelled? How does a rich kid like Willy wind up getting expelled?"

"By burning down the English department."

"What!"

He shrugged. "By burning down the English department."

It didn't make any more sense the second time.

I was frowning. "But Willy wasn't there during the sixties, was he? I mean, he couldn't've been in the SDS or . . . ?"

"This was not a case of student unrest or protest or what-have-you. Willy and his English prof had a disagreement, I think over whether Willy had cheated on a test and plagiarized his term paper."

It still seemed crazy. I was shaking my head.

"So," Brackett continued, "he burned down the English department building with the help of his friend Ernesto Vargas. They were caught and booted out."

"Booted into jail, you mean."

Brackett loved this. His smile was like the Mona Lisa's. "No. We're back to your first comment. How does a rich kid get expelled from college? Answer: by doing something that would get anybody else serious jail time. His dad has a lot of money to throw around, remember. You oughta to see the *new* English department building they put up . . ."

"Wait a minute. This is another *fire* . . ."

"Your shrewd reportorial instincts never fail to impress, Peterson. And what does the name Ernesto Vargas suggest?"

"Would he happen to be South American?" I asked.

"You're simply a genius," he said smugly.

"A fire back then . . . a fire at Beekman's . . . a college friend from South America . . . a South American assassin . . ."

"Exactly."

"So where the hell is Vargas *now*?"

He held his hands up, palms out, as if to say "Who knows?" "My sources haven't been able to track him down yet."

"What about your pal, Sam Smotherman? Maybe at least *he'd* remember Vargas from Yale."

He nodded. "Good thought. Didn't Sam give you his card?"

I nodded, dug it out of my purse. Brackett took it, thanked me, and went to the phone and touch dialed.

"By the way, I dressed like this 'cause I figured this is how you're supposed to dress at these pickup places. I didn't want to stand out or anything."

He shook his head. "No, you wouldn't want to do that. You'd want to be nice and inconspicuous. . . . Yes! Sam Smotherman, please. . . . Sam? Hey, it's Pete. Thanks for dinner the other night. . . . Sorry about the after-dinner entertainment. You seemed a little shook up. You okay now? . . . Can't keep a good man down. Say, could you check up on an old Yalie for me? Guy who was there at the same time as Willy Chess. Ernesto Vargas. . . . Not Bargas, *Vargas* with a 'V' like Victor. . . . Doesn't sound familiar, huh? Well, could you check on it, anyway? I'm gonna be in and out, so if you come up with anything. . . . Great! I'm still at the Mill Creek Inn, but you can always leave word at my office with Jeannie. If Jeannie's away from her desk, ask for Evans."

Brackett covered the phone with a hand.

"He wants to know, if he finds Vargas, will we clue him in on what we're working on?"

"No way," I said.

He uncovered the phone. "You got it, pal. Thanks a million."

He hung up, and I said, "I'm not going to share anything with that guy. I wouldn't trust him as far as I could throw him—he's a political hired gun, a lobbyist and a . . ."

He waggled a lecturing finger again. "Peterson, rule number four: If somebody's helpin' you out, always tell 'em what they want to hear."

"Oh. Lie, you mean."

"Little white lies never hurt anybody."

"Like in your book?"

He grinned. "You been reading it?"

"No! Shouldn't we get going?"

He reached for his tan suede jacket. "Listen, why don't I meet you at this 'Ruby's.' You take the car, I'll take a cab. If they *have* cabs in Spring Creek."

"Why are we doing that?"

He was shrugging into the jacket. He looked good in it, but I didn't let my expression say I thought so.

He said, "Like you said, this is a pickup joint, and we're both trying to score in our separate ways, aren't we? So we shouldn't arrive together."

He opened the door for me and I went out into the hall.

"See ya later," he said, and shut the door.

Ruby's Bar and Grill was a sprawling, noisy country-western bar doing a lively Friday night business—the kind of place where they serve baskets of peanuts and you toss the shells on the floor, where a raucous country-western band plays, and couples do the two-step. With the smell of seared cow flesh hanging heavily in the air, it was not a place for vegetarians (even of the modified eat-fish-and-fowl variety like me) and was a meat market in more ways than one.

This was Spring Creek's favorite singles bar, although I could see that the problem discussed by the girls in the ladies' room back at Chess Chemical was real. The females here outnumbered the men probably three to one.

I found myself a seat at the bar next to Kim—who had looked nice in a lab coat, but was borderline stunning in a low-cut black dress, her glasses gone, and her long-lashed dark eyes looking lovely in contacts. On the high wooden stool next to Kim was her redheaded friend from work—whose name turned out to be Darlene, and who wore an off-the-shoulder pink sweater and jeans.

These women meant business.

I had made enough small talk to get accepted, at least tentatively, into their circle. A bartender—a cute blond guy probably around twenty-five—came over and asked "Kimmy" for an introduction.

"This is Robin," Kim said, gesturing to me. "Robin, this is Mike—oh, *excuse* me . . . *Michael*. Robin's thinking of moving to Spring Creek."

"Do it! Always room for another lovely lady—"

"Right!" Darlene said. "Like a four-to-one ratio isn't enough to give you poor guys a break!"

"Hey," he said, wiping the bar clean in front of us and smiling slyly, "what's wrong with an embarrassment of riches?"

He laughed and moved down the bar.

"Don't you just hate grad students?" Kim asked.

"Is that true?" I asked. "Four women to every man?"

"It's depressingly true. Look around you."

I already had.

"Hey Dixon!" Kim called to a husky, nice-looking man of maybe thirty sitting across the bar. "What are you doin' here? Didn't your wife just have a baby?"

The guy raised his beer glass, and shrugged. "I'm celebratin'!"

Kim turned to me with her pretty mouth twisted into a humorless smile. "That's the trouble with small towns. Small *one-company* towns. These are for the most part the same faces I see every day at work. I know their problems, at work, at home. . . . I know who they're sleeping with, at work, at home."

I leaned in. "So, tell already."

Kim was pointing to another middle-aged man— to whom Darlene had just wandered over to flirt with—and seemed about to dish, when something else caught her attention.

"Well, lordamercy," she said, breathless, her dark eyes large. "Maybe I *did* win the lottery at that."

I followed her gaze to the front entry.

Peter Brackett had just stepped inside. A hostess had eagerly greeted him to offer a table, but he smiled, waved her off, and headed for the bar. He looked good in that dark suede coat and jeans, though not so good that every woman in the place ought to be following him with eager, greedy eyes.

But they were. Funny what a shortage of men will do.

"He is *hot*," Kim said.

"Well," I said, "room temperature, anyway."

Kim frowned at me. "You don't think that's one gorgeous man?"

I tried to remember my mission here and said, "He's a hunk, all right."

Kim leaned near me and whispered conspiratorially, "You know, I haven't been well-and-truly laid in so long that I can't remember what it's like."

"I'm sure it'll come back to you," I said.

Brackett took the seat Darlene had vacated, right next to Kim. He looked through me, then smiled at Kim.

"Hi," he said. "I'm David. I'm new in town."

"Kim," she said huskily, and offered her hand, as if she were royalty. "I can show you around if you like."

"We could start with the dance floor," Brackett said, with a seductive little grin.

It was a slow tune, a Billy Ray Cyrus number that the local country band managed to make sound even worse, and Brackett took Kim in his arms like they'd been lovers forever. He whispered in her ear and she laughed, and pretended to blush.

"Oh, brother," I said.

"Wanna dance?"

I swiveled on the stool and the guy standing there wore a tank top and jeans and had Fabio-type shoulder-length hair. He was a construction worker, probably, trying to look like a hunk and, even if he wasn't my type, succeeding at it.

Plus, he was handy.

Kim was playing with the hair at the back of Brackett's neck.

"Love to," I told Fabio.

At least the guy smelled good, and he had an incredible, muscular body. We slowly swayed to the awful music. I pretended to be really into it, and pretended not to notice Kim planting a big wet one on Brackett's lips, and particularly pretended not to notice that even though he was being kissed, his eyes were on me.

The song hadn't ended when I saw Kim lead Brackett off the dance floor. They went to the bar where she retrieved a light jacket and her purse, and then they were out the door.

"What's your name?" Fabio whispered in my ear.

"Bill," I said. "I won't feel comfortable with my feminine name till I have the final operation."

He let go of me and moved away quickly, his eyes as big as his pecs.

And then I was out of there.

16

A Ride in the Country

___

BYLINE: Peter Brackett

The cool night air felt refreshing as I walked from Kim's bungalow to the all-night diner where I'd arranged to meet Peterson. The place was empty except for the snoozing short-order cook behind the counter—and Peterson asleep in a booth.

I tapped her on the shoulder, very gently, but she bolted awake.

"Brackett!" She sat up, wiping the sleep from her mouth, her eyes. "What time is it, anyway?"

I slid in across from her. "Little after four. Guess I kind of lost track of time."

Her eyes widened with sarcasm. "Kind *of*. Maybe we ought to go back to the hotel, and you can fill me in on the gruesome details at breakfast." She got the car keys out of her purse. "I'll drive—just because I'm a woman, that doesn't mean I always have to be the *passenger*."

I leaned forward. "Peterson, you're assuming I slept with her. Did you ever consider that maybe I didn't?"

"Excuse me? I missed the part where I asked you if you slept with that little bimbo. I also missed the part where I gave a damn."

"I didn't sleep with her. I told her I respected her too much."

"Oh, please!"

"She's had a hard life, and I just listened. Which is what I do. That's part of being a reporter—"

"Spare me the lessons and rules right now. How you choose to get your information is your business. If you want to tomcat your way to a story—"

"Tomcat?"

"Did you lift her security pass, at least?"

"I didn't get the chance. She was with me practically all the time. Frankly, half the time she was all over me."

"Thanks for sharing," Peterson said crisply.

"Hey, *not* sleeping with her was maybe the hardest field work this reporter's ever done."

"Do I look like your damn roommate? Did I look like I want to hear this crap?"

She wasn't and she didn't. Besides, why was I justifying my actions to her, anyway?

"You're right," I said. "I apologize. You want a cup of coffee before we go back to the hotel?"

"I don't drink coffee. Like Beekman, remember?"

"Sorry. Some tea, then. I've got something to show you."

I got out the photo I'd managed to lift from the

end table back at Kim's. It depicted Kim surrounded by co-workers in lab coats, all grins as they gathered around a big birthday cake.

"Kim's surprise birthday party last year," I explained. "The bald guy in glasses is the late Darryl Beekman, Sr."

"And there's our friend Willy Chess," she said, pointing to him in the picture.

"Next to him is Alexander Hervey."

She looked at me curiously. "You say that like it matters."

"It does. Hervey is the Chess research scientist who developed LDF in tandem with Beekman." I scooched out of the booth. "I'm gonna get that coffee. . . Excuse me."

Not wanting to wake the cook, I got behind the counter and poured myself a cup. Chocolate-frosted donuts beneath a plastic lid beckoned. I lifted the lid off and helped myself to a couple.

"You want one?" I asked, holding one up.

She shook her head, making her hair shimmer over her shoulders. "No thanks. I try not to eat after eleven P.M. Eating when your body's inactive is bad for the metabolism, plus five'll get you ten those donuts were deep fat fried, and saturated fats are death. But don't let me stop you."

I sighed heavily and put both donuts back. "You're as much fun as a trip to the dentist."

"That's another thing eating those donuts'll get you."

I slid back into the booth, sipped my coffee, and glared at her. "Not a word about caffeine!"

"So," she said, "why haven't we heard about Alexander Hervey before?"

"I'm not sure. Maybe because Willy has kept him out of the picture."

"How so?"

"Promoted him, due to the success of LDF. Made him the head of a new research facility outside of Las Vegas."

"Bought him off, you mean."

"Maybe temporarily."

She frowned over her tea. "What do you mean?"

"Couple months ago," I said, "Hervey found out he had cancer. Kim says the grapevine at work says Hervey's terminal. Hanging on by a thread."

Her eyes were glazed in thought. Then she said, "I wonder why they didn't buy *Beekman* off with a transfer and a promotion?"

"According to Kim," I said, "they tried. He turned 'em down flat."

"Interesting."

"You know what I think?"

"What?"

"I think when all was said and done, after all the research on LDF was in, and all that money spent, something wasn't kosher."

She was nodding. "So Willy goes to Beekman, and Hervey . . ."

"Offers them cushy jobs and lots o' dough," I said, "to fudge the test results."

"Hervey accepts," she said, "takes the Vegas gig, but . . ."

"Beekman takes a pass, quits Chess . . ."

"Taking the *real* test results along for the ride," she said.

"And just in case some unforeseen 'accident' might occur—like that fatal coffeemaker fire, for instance—Darryl, Sr., sends Darryl, Jr., a copy of those test results."

"Works for me," she said. Then she pressed on: "Willy finds out, panics, and calls in his old firebug pal from south of the border, Ernesto Vargas."

"Money like this could renew many an old friendship."

She was shaking her head, looking glum. "I know I should feel good about this. . . . We're making all the pieces fit . . . but this is so sick. Wasn't mercury in fish and Alar on apples enough? Must we foist contaminated milk on the public? Is nothing sacred?"

"Sure," I said, "the almighty dollar."

She thought about that, and I thought about something else.

"You do realize," I said, "that there's only one person who can confirm or deny our suspicions."

A smile tickled half her face. "Does this mean we're going to Vegas?"

I grinned and shrugged. "If we're wrong, the worst that could happen is we wind up at a Wayne Newton show."

"Please God, don't let us be wrong."

We walked across the parking lot. Fog had started to roll in.

"You drive," she told me, handing me the keys. "I hate driving even two blocks in pea soup like this."

"All right, then," I said archly. "Let a *man* do it."

She allowed herself to laugh at that as I got in behind the wheel and she buckled up next to me. I pulled out onto the two-lane highway.

"Brother," she said, leaning back in her seat and yawning, "am I *dead*."

"No," someone said. "But you *could* be."

He was in the backseat. How he got there, I

didn't know, and he didn't offer the information. Not that the Mustang would be hard to spot.

He was thin and dark. Was this Peterson's "cadaverous" man? Probably not—this man with a gun (and he did have a gun, a .38 revolver with a four-inch barrel that was kissing Peterson's temple, at the moment) was too handsome to be described that way. He wore black, like any good assassin, but his accessories were Western.

We were at the hotel.

"Don't pull in," he said. "Just keep going. Head out of town."

The highway was a desolate stretch of concrete running through a countryside that was now entirely blanketed with fog.

"You have something that doesn't belong to you," he said quietly, "and I've been asked to get it back."

I didn't know what the hell he was talking about. I glanced sharply at Peterson, whose terrified eyes looked at me past the gun barrel at her head. Her eyes assured me she'd held nothing back, either.

The test results.

For some reason, the bad guys thought *we* had the duplicate set of test results, the ones that had supposedly been in Darryl Beekman's briefcase, which was already in the hands of the goddamn bad guys. So what made them think *we* had them?

"Keep it under sixty," he said, finally taking the gun away from Peterson's temple. "I'll tell you when and where to pull over."

With two of us, he had a lot of leverage. He could shoot one, which would certainly make the other one talk. Only I didn't think either Peterson or I knew anything he wanted to hear.

Visibility was damn near zero. I sat up over the

steering wheel, trying to make out the center line. I glanced at the Western killer as he sat in the backseat.

"This gives me a definite sense of *deja vu*," I said.

"What?" Peterson said, glaring at me. *This is no time for wisecracks*, her eyes said.

"I read about something almost exactly like this," I said, "in a paperback I read in college."

"Don't talk unless spoken to," he said.

"You don't get it," I said. "*I'm* the designated driver. What was it the guy in that paperback did? I remember . . ."

And I floored it.

"What are you doing?" Peterson blurted.

"Slow down, you son of a bitch," our passenger almost screamed, "or I'll blow you away right fucking now!"

"Try it. And try to imagine this car going out of control at this speed—"

"I'll *shoot* her!"

"She's not my girlfriend," I said. "She's the competition! She blackmailed me into bringing her along. If you want to shoot her, shoot her! Do me a favor!"

He was freaking back there, but he wasn't shooting.

The speedometer was climbing—we'd long ago passed 90; we were heading for 125.

That was when I yanked the wheel around, with a screech that could've woken the dead, and flew over the divider, and drove directly into the fog and the wrong lane. If anybody else was dumb enough to be out in this, and this was their lane, they might be in for an unfortunate surprise.

"Are you crazy?" the assassin was shouting. My

quick 180-degree turn had tossed him around in that backseat like shaking up a box of Chiclets. Only he still had the gun in hand. Unfortunately.

A pair of enormous headlights emerged from the fog, bearing right down on us, and I said, "Hold on, Peterson!" as the lights revealed themselves as belonging to the biggest damn bus Greyhound ever made.

"Peter!" she screamed.

First time she ever called me that.

The sound of the Greyhound's air horn was like the mournful wail of a huge dying beast. It filled my ears like the bus was filling my eyes (Peterson was covering hers) as I swerved away at the last second, yanking the wheel around again, sailing back over the divider and into the other lane.

Or that was the object of my effort.

The result was a wild spin that made a top of the Mustang. Peterson and I survived the dizzying ride, but our poor passenger in the leather outfit got his head smashed—first in this side window, then in the other, spiderwebbing the glass, and knocking the gun out of his hand and the consciousness from his person.

Peterson plucked the gun from him like Annie Oakley and gave me a smile, just before the Mustang skidded sideways onto the shoulder and slid to a stop against an embankment.

"Here's where you get off, amigo," I said, and nodded to Peterson, who had a gleam in her eyes as she reached back, unlocked the back door, and shoved our rider out of the car.

He didn't thank us for the ride, being out cold at the moment. He just rolled down to the bottom of the gully, where he could sleep some more, in peace.

"Maybe next time he'll remember to buckle up," Peterson said.

She pulled the door shut with a slam. She had a wild look—both wasted and wired.

Then she frowned. " '*Shoot* her?' 'Do me a *favor*?' "

"You're welcome," I said, and backed up the car, got onto the highway, and drove back into the fog.

In what I hoped was the right lane. I was kind of losing track. . . .

17

Detour

—

BYLINE: Sabrina Peterson

Branches were slapping against the windshield of the Mustang, as if we were running a gauntlet. Brackett was doing the best he could under these conditions, which is to say the thickest fog imaginable and driving a car whose reverse gear no longer worked down a narrow dirt country road, which maybe we weren't even on anymore, considering the foliage whipping our windshield.

Something had happened, apparently, to the gears or transmission or whatever, one of the times Brackett had driven the car up and over the center divider, during our high-speed episode with the wild-West assassin. And when the car had done its impression of a twirling dreidel, we'd emerged in a fog not just literal, but figurative, with no sense of direction, not even knowing if we were in the right lane.

When a car's headlights came toward us like white swords out of the haze, that provided a major clue.

Brackett pulled down this dirt road, thinking at first it was just an access inlet into a field, planning to just to back up and turn around.

And that was when we discovered the Mustang's reverse gear didn't work.

So we went with the gear that did work—drive—moving forward, hoping to find other intersecting roads and eventually wind our way back to Spring Creek, or at least to some city, town, village, or hamlet.

"Maybe we should just stop at a farmhouse," I offered.

He was hunched so far over the wheel, his nose practically touched the windshield. "If you see one, let me know."

"Are we going downhill?"

"In every sense," he said.

"This is getting steep. Careful!"

"I'm going about two miles an hour! How much more—"

He didn't finish this thought, because an ear-filling scraping sound interrupted him—part clunk, part metallic whine, with a little splash mixed in, as we lurched to a sudden stop that jolted us forward.

We just sat there for a long awful moment.

Then I asked, innocently, "Did we hit something?"

He looked at me with narrowed eyes, possibly considering hitting something else. Hands on the wheel, his expression somberly intense as he stared out into the swirling gray before us, he pressed the gas pedal to the floor.

The sound of our wheels spinning impotently told a hopeless story.

Without a word, we both opened our doors, to assess the situation, and water came rushing in.

"Better get out!" he advised, doing so himself, but I had already taken the initiative, and soon we were on either side of the Mustang, standing in a half foot of water in the bed of a stream.

The nose of our rental vehicle was lodged between two boulders.

There were other rocks in the bed of the stream, and we stepped across some of them to the nearest embankment. Still wearing last night's little black mini, I had my high heels in hand, and my purse on its strap over my shoulder.

We sat on the embankment, catching our breath, not saying anything much.

"Look on the bright side," I said.

"There's a bright side?"

"Sure. The bad guys don't know where we are."

"True. Also, we don't know where we are."

The fog was clearing, and the sun came up behind us, lovely shades of orange, yellow, and even purple streaking through the trees of a wooded area nearby.

"Spring Creek ought to be that way," I said, pointing toward the sunrise.

He squinted into the light. "You sure?"

"Sun rises in the east, doesn't it?"

At last I'd found a subject we had no argument about.

We trudged across a field, and into the wooded

area. Half an hour later, that's where we still were, pushing our way through the underbrush.

Brackett was leading the way. Without glancing back at me, he said, "What do you think our passenger meant when he said we had something that didn't belong to us?"

"I don't know. You don't suppose Beekman's test results weren't in that briefcase, do you?"

"Suppose they weren't. How does that make *us* have 'em?"

"Do you think Danny Brown could have taken out the test results and hidden them somewhere?"

"In his crash pad? The bad guys have torn that place apart by now, looking. *You* were in that theater."

I bristled. "Are you suggesting *I* have the test results? That I've been withholding them?"

"Do you? Have you?"

Angry, I walked faster, taking the lead as we pressed on through a thicket of young trees. I let them snap back and hit Brackett.

"Ouch," he said. "I was just asking."

Before long we were out of the woods.

And into the swamp.

"Do they *have* swamps in Wisconsin?" I asked him.

"You're a reporter," he said, as he sloshed through the grassy, marshy terrain. "What do *you* think?"

"I think I can't believe I'm still in this dress. I'm starting to feel like Ginger on *Gilligan's Island*."

"At last," he said, "a common cultural reference point. . . . Wait a minute, would you?"

"What?"

He had stopped to lean against a tree. He was

taking a stone out of his shoe. "Am I nuts or did you say you knew where we headed?"

"Is that a two-part question? We're lost. Okay? I screwed up, and we're lost. But we're never going to find Alexander Hervey if we keep stopping every five minutes."

"Oh, are we headed to Nevada, now?"

"I don't know. I only know one thing for sure."

"What's that?"

"That's poison ivy you're leaning against."

He jumped away from the tree.

"Three leaves on a cluster," I said, trudging onward.

He said something under his breath.

"Okay, then," I said. "Next time I *won't* tell you."

Finally we emerged into an open field. The grass was tall, possibly grazing land, but no cattle were in sight. What *was* in sight was the sun: The cool fall weather we'd been enjoying for days and days had picked this particular moment on this particular morning to turn into summer.

I tied my hair up with a string of stem and leaves. My dress was ripped here and there, but otherwise I was in good shape. From my purse I took my bottle of sunscreen and began applying it to my arms.

"You want some?" I asked him. "It's paba free."

"No thanks," he said. His smirk wasn't very friendly. He looked like he was on a safari in his T-shirt, with his pants rolled up, his shirt off and wrapped like a turban around his head.

"It's up to you," I said, holding the sunscreen bottle over my open purse, giving him one last chance.

"What *don't* you have in that thing? That's not a purse, it's Batman's utility belt."

"I don't have a compass, if that's what you're wondering. You really should take the sunscreen, Brackett—four out of every ten Americans get skin cancer before the age of—"

"Peterson, cut me a break, would ya? I've had it up to here with your new-age health tips. Don't eat bacon—high cholesterol; don't eat maraschino cherries—red dye number three. Don't eat *donuts*—saturated fats. Do you know what I would give for a fucking donut right now?"

I would've eaten one myself.

"Then you don't want the sunscreen?" I asked.

"No. I don't want the sunscreen."

"Okay, then."

I put it away.

We moved on. The field seemed as endless as the sun was warm. Hot.

"Peterson," he said, behind me, "you know where I'd be right now, if it wasn't for you?"

"You're going to tell me, aren't you?"

"On the L.A. leg of my book tour. Sitting around the pool at some fancy-ass hotel, giving interviews, staring at starlets, and eating a Cobb salad—with extra bacon."

"And you can say that with a straight face?"

"Why not?"

"I don't know. It's embarrassing. Shallow."

"Shallow? Embarrassing? I'll tell you what's embarrassing—traipsing through cow pastures with my shirt wrapped around my head!"

"There's some more trees up ahead."

"Great! Wonderful! Are they new trees, or old

trees? Or we walking around in circles, or in one long pointless straight line?"

"You're losing it, Brackett."

"I lost it the day I let this story take hold of me." He was shaking his head, muttering. "They kill Beekman, but he'd already given what they were after to his son. We think it's some test results, but we're not *really* sure. Then they kill the son, 'cause he has whatever-it-is, only he *doesn't* have it. They thought he had it, but he didn't. They think *we* have it, but we don't. Is it hidden? Would we know it if we saw it? In any case, you don't have to have it or even know what it is to get killed for it by these people. Why would I rather be sitting around a pool staring at starlets, when I can wander through the countryside with you, contemplating my own meaningless life and death?"

"Maybe you're right."

"Of course, I'm right!"

"Maybe it's hidden."

He groaned. Stopped. I stopped, too, and looked at him, and he was shaking his head, his eyes wide.

"You're actually having a good time, aren't you?" he said, incredulous. "You're *enjoying* this goddamn story!"

"Aren't you?"

He gestured to himself, to the shirt wrapped on his head, his rolled-up pants legs, to the nearly shredded shoes that had once been expensive loafers. His eyes seemed a little desperate.

"Do I *look* like a man enjoying himself? We're lost, Peterson! *I'm* lost!"

Now it was my turn to waggle a lecturing finger in *his* face.

"You look like a man who's *found* himself, Brack-

ett. You *were* lost—book parties, 'scoring' with group-
ies, frivolous columns, celebrity bullshit—until you
met me, and remembered what being a reporter was
like. You could have quit any damn time you wanted,
but no—you stayed with it, because this is the story
of a lifetime, and no matter how you might protest,
you know in your heart of hearts that you'd rather be
an ace reporter than an also-ran novelist."

He frowned, and seemed to be gathering his
thoughts for a response at least as long as my tirade,
when his nose crinkled and he began to sniff the air.
He looked like a rabbit. A rabbit in a makeshift
turban, that is.

"You smell that?" he said, eyes bright, a little-kid
smile curving his mouth. "You can *hear* it, too!"

"What?"

"Some reporter," he said, and he began moving
quickly though the trees and I followed him and
there it was.

The loveliest lake in the state of Wisconsin.

It stretched out before us, a glimmering, shimmering vision of God's best work. Under a sky as
washed-out a blue as well-worn jeans, the rippling
surface of the lake was a gray-blue that complimented perfectly the brilliant greens of pines all
around.

"First dibs," I said.

"Huh?" he said.

The water was as cool as it looked—not cold, but
cool, the perfect antidote to the blistering heat. The
last time I'd gone skinny-dipping was in a similar
lake at Camp Wopacotapotalong when I was a little
girl—a pleasant memory, but in the future nothing
would top this.

Brackett had promised to give me a good ten

minutes, and warn me when he got back. He'd gone looking for breakfast—if anyone could find chocolate donuts in this forest, it would be him—and came back holding his front shirt tail in front of him, as a makeshift basket.

"What have you got there?"

"Wild berries!" he called.

"Are you sure they're edible?"

"I was planning on having *you* try 'em first!"

I laughed. It echoed across the lake. "Turn around! I'm getting out."

He stood just beside the little pile of my clothes on the grassy bank—my poor tattered mini and some undergarments. He had his back to me as I bent down to pick them up, and they were in my hands and not even partly on me when the sound of branches cracking underfoot told us we had company.

From the sound of it, a lot of company!

Damn—had someone tracked us here?

I huddled behind Brackett, looking over his shoulder at the wooded area from which the sound of tramping feet emanated, and then there they were: every damn Boy Scout in the world!

"Rescue!" Brackett said, stepping forward toward the boys, who were emerging from the thicket—leaving me completely exposed.

And then I was looking at at least two dozen, wide-eyed, mouths-hanging-open, prepubescent faces. Several of the scouts were hauling a canoe over their heads, which they dropped on their heads with a *thunk* upon seeing me.

Their first naked woman.

It was only a fraction of a second, but it was a

fraction of a second those young men would carry with them a lifetime. Me, too.

I grabbed Brackett, making a human shield of him.

"Be nice," I whispered urgently.

But the grin he threw back at me wasn't nice at all. "What was that about 'also-ran novelist?'"

"Did I say that? What do I know? I never even read your book."

"I thought I saw you reading it in your room."

"When?"

"When I looked through the keyhole between our rooms at the Lake Mill Inn."

"You louse!" I didn't mention that I'd had a peek or two at him myself, the same way.

"That's no way to talk," he said, and took a step forward. I didn't let him get away—I shadowed his every movement, his every step, clutching him around the waist.

"Hi fellas," I said, peeking around Brackett's shoulder at them. "Hey! Isn't that a water mocassin?"

They didn't flinch. Or blink, for that matter.

Brackett was moving toward them. So was I, in toy-soldierlike lockstep with the big bum. I was begging him not to do this, to stop, but he pressed on.

We were perilously near the little, bug-eyed, budding voyeurs now.

"This is what they meant by 'be prepared,'" Brackett was telling them, and they grinned and nodded eagerly.

"Okay," I said, "I'm *reading* your damn book."

"And?"

"I don't have an opinion yet—I'm only fifty pages in."

"Boys, are any of you working on your biology merit badge?"

"It's cute!"

"Cute?" he asked, looking back with an arched eyebrow. Then to the boys he said, "You can't beat a nature hike for real education. Who's got a camera?"

Every damn one of them pulled out an Insta-matic.

"Be prepared," Brackett said.

"No . . ." I began.

Then Brackett laughed gently and said, "Guys— back off and give my friend some privacy. And then we're gonna need some of that helpin'-little-old-la-dies-across-the-street assistance you fellas are so famous for. . . ."

The ride back to Spring Creek on the school bus that had brought the scouts into the wilderness was uneventful. I sat in back, and of course had my clothes on now, though every little eye was still on me, knowingly.

18

Shotgun Wedding

—

BYLINE: Peter Brackett

Glitter Gulch is what they call Fremont Street, and Peterson and I had taken a cab here from McCarren Airport. Early this afternoon, at the Mill Creek Inn, I'd called the *Chronicle* and had Jeannie book us a Las Vegas flight out of Spring Lake, as well as reservations at the Union Plaza.

Now, as we basked in the perpetual neon noon of downtown Vegas at night, it was hard to believe that just this morning we'd been trudging through the boonies of Wisconsin. But here we were, in all our jetlagged glory, and here Vegas was, in all its glitz and garish splendor.

On the other hand, if the neon had been any brighter, I might have asked Peterson for that sunscreen (I had as yet to admit to her that my face was hot from this morning's sun exposure).

We hadn't been to the hotel yet, though it was within sight. Peterson had tugged me into a Western-style clothing shop, and before I knew what had hit me, we were back out on the tourist-teeming street dressed in kitschy Western garb, with the clothes we'd worn stuffed into shopping bags, carry-ons over our shoulders.

"We look like Roy Rogers and Dale Evans," I said, studying our reflections in the store window.

"We look like tourists," she said, "and that's the point. We want to blend in."

I was still looking at myself. "The social situation does not exist where this shirt would blend in. And as for these boots . . ."

"Shit."

"What do you mean by that, exactly?"

"Roy—we have company."

Then I saw the reflection in the store window—not hers, not mine, but that of a tall, thin man in a khaki suit. He had angular features that might best be described as cadaverous.

"That's him?" I asked. "The guy outside Danny Brown's apartment building?"

He was standing just across the street, with the neon backdrop saying JACKPOT just over his head. His stare was steady and undisguised, and if that cadaverous countenance of his were any more sinister, I might have laughed. Or screamed.

"That's him."

I took her by the hand and we walked swiftly along the crowded sidewalk—nobody but us was in a hurry, since after all nobody in Vegas was ever in a hurry, except to lose their money—and when I glanced back, I could see the thin man zigzagging quickly across the street, through and around pedestrians. He was locked onto us like a heat-seeking missile.

"Brackett!" she called. "Watch out!"

I'd been looking behind us and didn't realize we were about to cross the path of a passel of elderly tourists who were filing off their charter bus. Suddenly we were awash in a sea of seniors, but that was okay, at least momentarily, because they provided a sort of protection. We did our best to blend in—I was aging fast—and stayed with the pack as it continued down the street in search of a bingo parlor.

Then we were waiting at the corner, and the intersection was swarming with cars fore and aft, and the thin man was coming up the sidewalk after us, his hand inside his khaki jacket.

I didn't think he had an itch.

So I left Peterson behind with the bingo brigade and bolted out into the intersection, dodging and dancing and weaving, then planted my feet firmly and held out my hand like a crossing guard, and motioned gallantly for the old folks to cross.

With traffic halted, the seniors sauntered safely across, their eyes huge as they contemplated the gigantic neon BINGO sign luring them forward. One old gal even slipped a chip worth a whole buck in the pocket of my gaudy western shirt.

Peterson crossed with the pack, but stopped midway to stay with me, and when the thin man was about to step off the curb, I released traffic, dashing across with Peterson keeping pace at my side as the intersection immediately filled with cars and taxis, pinning the thin man at the opposite corner.

I glanced back, once, and saw him in pursuit

dodging cars, his cadaverous face glowering; but we were moving faster, and we rounded a corner and across the way a blue stucco building with pink neon beckoned. Amid neon hearts, pulsing with a reassuringly regular beat, were the words LITTLE CHAPEL OF DREAMS.

Yanking Peterson by the wrist, we started across the street.

"Where are you taking me, Brackett?"

"We're goin' to the chapel," I said, and slipped inside. We stood with our backs to a wall, catching our breath. The waiting room area was white, with lots of latticework and artificial flowers, and Elvis (or a reasonable facsimile) was singing "Blue Hawaii" over a mildly distorting sound system.

In the more churchlike adjacent chapel area, a ceremony was under way.

A groom in jeans and a tux jacket and a bride in a red dress and a wedding veil were receiving their vows from a middle-aged, crew-cut man in glasses and an Hawaiian shirt that made my western ensemble seem the epitome of good taste.

Still with my back to the wall, I glanced around and through the chapel's front window could see the thin man going quickly in the office of the glitzy pink palace across the street whose neon identified it as the Honeymoon Hotel.

The newlyweds were kissing. I couldn't help thinking of Tim and Amy Weiss, and what the same people who were after us had done to their young lives.

The preacher (or justice of the peace or whatever the hell he was—Hawaiian Orthodox, for all I knew) beamed up at us over his Bible, calling out, "You kids up next?"

"No," Peterson said, "we're just browsing . . ."

I glanced out the window and the thin man was crossing the street, headed our way. Goin' to the chapel. . . .

"What a great little kidder," I said, taking Peterson by the arm. "You bet we're next."

I escorted her inside the chapel area, toward the altar, and she whispered, "This is a little *sudden*, isn't it?"

But our Hawaiian-shirted host had swung into full gear, even as a little middle-aged bridesmaid with a single blond braid down her back was stripping the newlyweds of their tux jacket and veil.

He was addressing us with a frighteningly glazed smile, and mad-scientist eyes behind his thick glasses; but at least his features weren't cadaverous.

"And what accouterments would you lovebirds like this evening? We can provide flowers, fresh or silk, a wide variety of music, prerecorded or live. You understand, for live flowers and live music, we'd have to schedule you for at least an hour from now."

"Spare no expense," I said, "just don't keep us waiting." I hugged Peterson to me; her eyes were a little wild. "We've been waiting for this moment for such a very long time . . ."

"Traditional couple, huh? You want a video?"

"Why not?"

His expression turned thoughtful. "Now, I can change into my western shirt. That would seem to suit your ensemble."

"No," I said, "let's keep it eclectic."

Then the preacher was handing me the tux jacket, which I slipped on (very loose—one size fits all), as his braided blond assistant was placing the veil on Peterson, covering her face. Good.

Not that there was anything at all wrong with Peterson's face; I just didn't want the thin man to pop in, "browsing," and instantly recognize us. In fact, I was wishing grooms wore veils.

The aging bridesmaid (actually, the braid was more milk maid) lifted a camcorder to her shoulder and began recording as the blessed event unfolded.

Our host thoughtfully asked, "You want the abridged, or the full boat?"

Another glance behind me revealed the thin man was now standing *right out front*—with his back to the chapel window. Thank God for small favors.

"I don't care," I said. "Just go for it."

"Now!" Peterson said.

She'd glanced back at the front window, too.

The preacher smiled. "Your sweetheart's changed her tune."

"Sneak another look," I whispered to her. "He won't recognize you in the veil."

She glanced back, then back at me. Her eyes behind the veil were alarmed. "He's peeking in the window . . ."

"Honey," the preacher said, addressing the bridesmaid, "the music, if you please."

Honey, a virtual one-woman band, didn't miss a beat shooting the video even as she leaned back to switch on a boom box perched on a ledge among some faux flowers behind her.

"I'll need your names," the preacher said.

"Peterson," she said.

"Brackett," I said.

"Peterson and Brackett," he began. "You have decided to unite your mutual love in holy matrimony. . . ."

I heard the door in the lobby open, letting in street sounds. Then it closed.

He was in.

"To make a commitment that will last a lifetime. . . ."

Which might not be much of a commitment.

". . . sacred moment you will cherish as long as you live. . . ."

I wished he'd quit rubbing it in our faces like that.

"Honey," the preacher was saying, "if you please—the rings."

A plastic baggie sailed through the air—Honey had a good arm—and the preacher caught it deftly. He opened it and removed the two gold bands. They weren't plastic—they were metal. Chances were we wouldn't be alive long enough for them to turn our skin green.

"And now I ask, do you Brackett, take this woman to be your lawful wedded wife, to cherish and protect, in good fortune and adversity alike?"

I sneaked a look behind me. The thin man was standing in the chapel's waiting area, staring our way. He hadn't heard our names. But we'd been stupid not to use false ones.

"Is that him?" she whispered.

"Yeah," I said.

"Fine," the preacher nodded, accepting that as my response, and said, "Do you, Peterson, take this man to be your lawful wedded husband . . ."

I whispered to her, "If he comes in the chapel, we're out that side exit."

". . . promising to cherish and protect him, whether in good fortune or adversity?"

"Okay," she said, answering me.

But that answer was good enough for the rev, who nodded again, and said, "And so, by the powers vested in me by the great state of Nevada . . ."

I wasn't listening to him; I was listening behind me, where—thank God!—I heard the sound of the door closing.

Peterson looked at me, beaming in relief.

"I now pronounce you man and wife!"

Confetti bombarded us suddenly—the ever-versatile Honey—and we gave each other identical wedding presents: astounded expressions.

"You may kiss the bride."

I gave her a peck on the cheek, and the preacher informed me that we'd just spent seventy-five dollars, but we should remember that the fee included a twenty-five-percent-off coupon at the Honeymoon Hotel across the street.

"Pay the man," my wife said.

I did.

They practically whisked the tux jacket off me and the veil off Peterson, and then we were stumbling toward that side exit, in a daze, when a deep voice called out to us.

"Don't forget your tape," Honey said, holding out the cassette.

19

Honeymoon in Vegas

BYLINE: Sabrina Peterson

The pink door with the numbered cupid swung open to reveal a fantasy bridal suite—but then, that was the only kind of suite the Honeymoon Hotel offered. Every suite, I felt sure, went something like this: heart-shaped bed with red satin spread, mirrored ceiling, light-pink lace curtains, deeper pink plush carpeting, pink champagne in an ice bucket. Faintly, in the background, romantic strings played "The Love Boat" theme.

We hadn't needed help with our bags—just two carryons and a couple of shopping bags—but the pink-uniformed bellboy showing us to paradise's door was part of the Honeymoon Hotel package. He unlocked the portal to ecstasy for us and Peter Brackett, showing exactly the charm and grace you might expect, walked right in, leaving the bellboy and me—his bride of a few minutes—standing in the hallway.

"Mr. Drummond," the bellhop said coyly, stepping into the room. "Aren't you forgetting something?"

"Oh. Yeah." He dug in his pocket and handed the bellboy a dollar.

"Thank you, sir, but that's not what I meant . . ."

Still standing out in the hall, I cleared my throat and made a gesture with my arms, as if I were rocking to sleep the world's largest baby. Brackett frowned in confusion and then, finally, got it.

He came out into the hall and lifted me into his arms and carried his bride over the threshold.

Even this was not enough for our pink-uniformed friend. He stood at the round light switch and, addressing his comments to Brackett, said, "Here's the dimmer for your lights—the switch that controls the degree of vibration for your bed is conveniently located on your bedstand. Would you like me to show you how the jacuzzi in our love tub works?"

"No thanks," Brackett said. "And much as I appreciate the guided tour, a buck is all you get."

The bellboy laughed as if that were a joke. Knowing Brackett, I didn't think it was.

"Now don't worry, Mr. Drummond," the bellboy said. "All of our rooms are one hundred percent soundproof."

Then he winked, threw a handful of rice at us, and was gone.

"Alone at last," I said.

We had decided not to use the Union Plaza reservations, because the Honeymoon Hotel was

safer: It was the one hotel in town that a certain
cadaverous stalker had already determined we were
not staying at.

Plus, we had the discount coupon from the Little
Chapel of Dreams.

Now Brackett was looking at me with what
seemed to be a tender expression. "Peterson . . . can
I ask you something? Something sort of personal?"

"No . . . no, go right ahead."

"Would you mind if I took the jacuzzi first?
After all that running, I'm afraid I worked up an
awful sweat."

When I came out of the bathroom after my turn with
the jacuzzi—wearing the pink terry robe that was,
yes, part of the Honeymoon Hotel package—I found
Brackett sitting on the edge of the round bed, using
the phone. He was wearing a terry robe, a blue one,
whose heart embroidered on the pocket matched the
one on mine.

Room service had arrived, while I was enjoying
the whirlpool, and several heart-shaped silver trays
awaited on a small table set for a candlelit supper.
Suddenly the hotel seemed less tacky. This was
almost elegant. At least for a girl from Santa Rosa
it was.

"You can't get *anything* on Ernesto Vargas?"
Brackett was saying into the phone, with not just a
little frustration. "Well, did Sam call? . . . Really?
Twice? . . . He came up empty, too? Well—keep at
it, Evans. Thanks. 'Bye."

He hung up and I came over and said, "No luck
on Vargas, huh?"

"Nope. Even Sam's striking out—can't find a
soul who knew Vargas at Yale, but he's gonna keep

trying. On the Alexander Hervey front, however, there is good news. Evans got me the unlisted number."

He held up a slip of paper.

"I'm gonna try him right now," he said.

But all Brackett got was an answering machine.

"Should I leave our number?" he asked me, cupping the receiver.

"Yes. Do it."

He left our number at the Honeymoon Hotel and asked Mr. Hervey to call ASAP.

"We're reporters from Chicago," he told the answering machine. "And with your help, we can blow the lid off the LDF cover-up."

He hung up.

"That should get his attention," Brackett said. "But it was a woman's voice on the answering machine."

"His wife?"

"I hope so." His expression lightened. "You hungry?"

"You remember the last time we ate, don't you? On the plane? The 'snack?'"

He shuddered. "I can't believe I actually flew coach. But that's all that was available."

"Now maybe you can identify with the little people better."

He stood and gestured toward the door. "You mind if I dim the lights? My eyes are killing me—besides, we can dine by candlelight like a real honeymooning couple."

"Why not?" I said.

We sat across from each other at the little table in the flickering glow of the tall pink candles. Even the white table cloth was elegant. Did I say the

Honeymoon Hotel was tacky? Forget that. "Elegant" is the word.

He was pouring me a glass of pink champagne. Then he poured himself some, and raised his glass in a toast.

"To the bravest girl I ever knew," he said.

"Who, me? Why? 'Cause I managed to stay alive till now?"

"No . . . because you married me."

We clinked glasses and began sipping. He lifted the silver tray off his meal and revealed a heart-shaped steak, heart-shaped fried potatoes, and a heart-shaped roll. Between us was a small plate with seven little heart-shaped pats of butter.

"I'm afraid to look at mine," I said, hand poised to lift the heart-shaped lid.

"Go for it."

But it was just a big salad.

I shrugged. "Guess they couldn't find a way to heart-shape this."

"It's a chicken Caesar. Check out the chicken."

The chunks indeed were heart-shaped. I began to giggle and Brackett, chewing a bite of his now deformed heart-shaped steak, was laughing, too.

Maybe elegant isn't the word, but the Honeymoon Hotel *was* fun.

I shook my head, studying the champagne bubbles in my glass. "You know, if someone had told me two weeks ago that I'd be marrying Peter Brackett—"

"If someone had told you *yesterday,* you'd've said they were nuts."

"Now here we are."

"Don't worry about it. I had Evans check."

"On what?"

"We can get this annulled in the morning."

"Oh. Oh! Well, that's . . . good. That's a relief. But I've broken my own record."

"How so?"

"A twelve-hour marriage. That's even shorter than my first one."

His expression was interested and sympathetic. "I didn't know you were married before."

"You find it hard to imagine someone marrying me under less than combat conditions?"

"No! Not at all. But it's that I'm sort of . . . particular about who my wives have been married to. Who was he?"

"Name's O'Connor. Of Peterson, Peterson, and O'Connor."

"Stupid question: any relation?"

I nodded. "My father and grandfather. They love Jimmy. Jimmy O'Connor, I mean. He's still extremely close to not only Dad, but my mom, too. Ridiculously close."

He cocked his head. "How do you mean?"

I laughed as if I thought what I was about to reveal was amusing. "Jimmy got remarried a couple months ago, and my parents were invited."

He reacted as if somebody had punched him. "They went to their ex-son-in-law's wedding?"

"They sure did. Hey, I don't wish him ill. He found the perfect wife for himself this time around. Great cook, terrific little housekeeper. Plus, he gets along better with all the Petersons than I do these days."

"I'd think they'd be proud of you."

"I guess."

He seemed to be studying me. "How long did it last? You and O'Connor."

"Ten months."

"That long?"

"Well, he moved out after seven, and we made a half-hearted attempt at counseling. After six months, I knew it was over. My fault."

"*Your* fault?"

"I blew the honeymoon."

His simle was warm. "I find that hard to accept— if you don't mind my saying so."

"I don't mind. But I did blow the honeymoon. See, we were supposed to take a cruise to Tahiti, but the local savings and loan went belly-up, and I had the inside track, and . . ."

"And you couldn't blow a front-page story. I don't blame you."

"You don't?"

He shook his head "no," but the gesture was an affirmative one. "He should've understood. Honeymoons can be postponed. Great stories have their own timetable."

I smirked, ate a bite of salad. "Where were you when I needed you?"

His smile was wry but also bittersweet. "Messing up my own marriage."

"Married life didn't suit you?"

"Oh, it suited me fine. It was my wife it didn't suit. She said I was never home. She said I loved the *Chronicle* more than I did her."

"That wasn't fair."

He grinned. "Sure it was. She was right."

I had to laugh. "Did she ever say, 'I'll never mean as much to you as some lead you're chasing down?'"

His eyes lighted up with immediate recognition. "Yes! She said she was jealous of the boys—"

"In the city room."

"Yeah!"

I shook my head, held my glass out for him to pour me some more champagne. "Funny," I said, "but there's one thing that's different about our respective marriages."

"Yeah?"

"It's a man/woman thing. Your wife was probably first attracted to you because of who you were, and what you did."

He began to nod emphatically, gesturing with his glass. "You're right. Then after we got married, she got *jealous* of it."

"In my case, though, Jimmy never admired me, or what I did. I was just a 'girl.' He put up with it when we were dating. And once we were married, he'd had enough."

Brackett was staring past me; his eyes were distant. Softly, he said, "She's married to a CPA now. Brilliant man. He has more sweaters than God."

I laughed. "And he's home every night."

"You bet. In front of the TV with the little woman."

"Safe. Secure. Normal."

"Brain-dead."

We both laughed.

I finished my second glass of champagne and said, "Well, considering my record, this may be my one and only honeymoon. So I might as well enjoy it."

I poured myself another glass.

"We'll sleep in shifts, of course," he said.

"What?"

"In shifts. Just in case your skull-face friend manages to track us down somehow. Or if we made a major blunder leaving our number on the Hervey's answering machine."

"Oh. Good idea. You want to take the first sleep shift?"

He shrugged. "No. That's okay. I got the jacuzzi first. You get some rest. Why don't we sleep four hours, trade off, then decide if we need a few more hours' sleep before trying to find the Hervey place."

"We're not going to wait for a call back?"

"No. If we haven't heard from Hervey by morning, we'll track down his address, somehow, and go out there."

"It all hinges on him, doesn't it?"

"I'm afraid so. Go to bed."

I practically collapsed on the bed. He came over and asked if I minded if he sat on the other side of the bed, reading, with the nightstand light on. He didn't want to disturb me.

"Go ahead," I said.

He began reading the new *Time* and I turned my back to him.

"Brackett?"

"Yeah?"

"A lot of guys would try to take advantage of a situation like this."

"I guess."

"I know I can trust you not to though."

"Right."

"Because I'm not your type. You don't . . . find me attractive."

He didn't say anything.

"What is it, exactly, that you don't like?" I asked. "I'm just curious. Not pretty enough? Too pretty? Too tall? Short? Hair color? Do I talk too much?"

"Go to sleep."

"You might be surprised to find that some men

find me reasonably attractive. I know you think I'm more trouble than I'm worth . . ."

"I don't feel that way about you, Peterson."

"You don't?"

"No."

"I don't feel that way about you, either, Brackett."

"You don't?"

"No."

Silence.

Then he said: "Are you at all interested in how I *do* feel?"

"Sure," I said, and turned to look at him, and he kissed me.

I guess maybe it was a kiss I'd been waiting for, even longing for, and as a reporter I strive for honesty, and I have to honestly tell you, this was honestly a kiss worth waiting for.

"That's a first for me," he said. He sounded almost breathless.

"What . . . what do you mean?"

"Never kissed a newspaperman before."

"How do you like it?"

He kissed me again. It was a soft, sweet kiss.

"I've been missing out," he said.

"This isn't going to change anything."

He kissed me again.

"I know," he said.

"I'm still the *Globe,* and you're . . ."

He kissed me again.

". . . the *Chronicle,*" he said. "I know, Sabrina, I know . . ."

"You called me 'Sabrina.'"

"It's your name."

"Peter . . . we're still the competition."

He kissed me again.

"Who do you think's winning?" he asked

He was kissing my neck and untying my terry robe when the goddamn phone rang.

It stopped us.

Then it rang again and kept ringing, and we exchanged a look that said we both knew he had to answer it, and he did. He fumbled for it, and said, "Hello." Then he held the receiver so I could listen.

It was a woman's voice. "This is Virginia Hervey. You left word about wanting to see my husband."

Brackett sat up. So did I.

"Yes, I . . ." he began.

"If you want to be safe, you should come now."

"Right now?"

"Right now," she said, and gave us the address.

And, so, soon—sooner, I think, than either of us would have preferred—we were getting dressed. I was trying on a pair of spike heels I'd found at the touristy clothing shop on Fremont Street.

"These are the kind of trashy shoes that drove my ex-husband crazy," I said, holding out my legs, showing off the new heels.

"They're not helping the sanity of your current husband, either," Brackett said. He was pulling on a pair of running shoes he'd bought at the same shop. I preferred him in the western boots I'd talked him into buying, but maybe considering what had been happening to us lately, running shoes weren't a bad idea.

"Hey," I said, "don't forget your wallet!"

And I plucked it off the nightstand and tossed it over on the bed by him. When the wallet landed, something fell partway out.

Kim's Chess Chemical security pass.

He *had* lifted it at her place last night!

And he hadn't told me.

Even now he was smoothly tucking the pass back inside the wallet, no doubt hoping I hadn't noticed it. Well, I sure as hell wasn't going to say anything. If that was the way he wanted to play it, fine by me.

He got off the bed, shoved his wallet in his back pocket, and offered me a hand, graciously, as if inviting me to waltz.

"Shall we, Mrs. Brackett?"

I nodded, and looked into his eyes and hoped all he saw there was love for him and enthusiasm for this story we were about to crack.

And not my heart breaking.

20

Rule Number Ten

——

BYLINE: Peter Brackett

$\mathbf{T}$he Hervey home was a rambling ranch-style on one of those quietly residential streets in Las Vegas that tourists never see. We parked our latest rental car across the way and started up a long walk through an immaculately attended lawn with occasional tasteful touches of rock and flower. The breeze from the desert was cool—deceptively soothing weather, considering what we'd been through of late.

We didn't even have to ring the doorbell. Virginia Hervey had been watching for us.

She was a small, attractive Asian woman in a sweater and slacks whose pastels were as cool as the evening. She might have been in her forties or even her sixties—I just couldn't tell. But she was a lovely, graceful woman, despite the fact that her brow was troubled and her greeting perfunctory. She hustled us inside like people she didn't want the neighbors to see.

She quietly led us through the house, as if it were a museum, not a home. The vintage of the place was probably 1950s, long before the Southwestern motif became fashionable, with a lot of attractive stonework and Japanese motifs, and colors echoing the cool pastels of her wardrobe.

"My husband is home now," she was saying, "because the doctors tell us there's nothing more they can do for him."

Not a museum, then—a hospital.

"I'm very sorry," Peterson said.

Her smile was heart-wrenching. "Thank you. Not every day is bad."

We had reached a closed door. She opened it carefully, as if there might be something volatile within that would go off if she acted otherwise.

But there was nothing at all volatile in the room—just a frail-looking, colorless man propped up with several pillows in the double bed. The only light was on the nightstand, next to a hardcover copy of the book *Powershift*, which was spread open, face-down, saving a place.

"Alex," Mrs. Hervey said, "those reporters from Chicago are here."

Alexander Hervey was possibly in his sixties, though he looked much older than that. His eyes were empty. As we guardedly moved toward him, I could tell Peterson thought at first that he was dead. She gave me a worried glance, but I shook my head "no." As eerie as the unacknowledging, unblinking eyes were, this man was not dead. The pulse in his crepey neck was apparent. His chest was rising and lowering. Not dead.

But not really alive.

Certainly not as alive as we needed him to be.

Mrs. Hervey sat on the edge of the bed. Her tender smile was a painfully poignant thing to have to witness. She took his hand and patted it gently.

"Alex, dear . . . they've come such a long way. . . . I know you *want* this . . . darling. . . ."

But it was no use.

Hervey didn't seem to know she was there, let alone two strangers from Chicago.

She walked us somberly back to the front door. An air of defeat accompanied us. Along the way we passed a booklined study with a cluttered desk and the open door to a bathroom.

We stood near the entry and she told us something, something that she had had to decide to tell us.

"I suppose . . . I should tell you . . ." she began.

"Please," I said.

"Someone phoned earlier, asking if you were coming to see me."

"Who?" Peterson asked.

"A man. He said he was a reporter, but when I asked him his name, and what paper he worked for, he hung up."

I traded wary expressions with Peterson.

"Some reporters will do that," I said, not wanting to alarm her.

But she shook her head—there was more.

"Then," Mrs. Hervey continued, "I saw someone parked across the street. This is not a busy neighborhood. We notice strangers. He sat there for a long time—hours—watching our house."

"Did you get a license number?" Peterson asked. "Could you describe the car?"

She shook her head. Her expression was almost sorrowful. "I'm sorry, but no. It was after dark, and our house sits well back away from the street, as you can see. I didn't want to make myself conspicuous. I just saw a car, and the shape of someone sitting in it . . . watching us."

"If that happens again," I told her, "you should call the police. Promise me you will."

She smiled, just a little, and said, "You're very considerate, Mr. Brackett."

Not something I'm often accused of.

Then she said, "You wanted to talk to my husband about Dr. Beekman, didn't you?"

A small ray of hope.

"Why, yes," I said, trying not to sound too damn eager. Nodding toward Peterson, I said, "We were confused as to why—after LDF was such a success—your husband was promoted, while at the same time Dr. Beekman left Chess Chemical."

"We're just wondering," Peterson picked up, "what the reason might be."

"Wondering?" she asked us both. Her eyes were sharp. "Or did you think you might know?"

I glanced at Peterson, and she nodded her permission.

"Actually," I said, "we *do* think we know. We just need something—somebody—to substantiate our theories."

Mrs. Hervey was listening, conveying the sense that she knew exactly we were talking about, but not offering anything further.

Peterson prompted her. "Mrs. Hervey, did your husband mention anything about Dr. Beekman? Did they, perhaps, have any disagreements? Particularly over the LDF research?"

Mrs. Hervey's smile was sad and sympathetic. "Never. They were good friends, trusted colleagues. I was hoping Alex could talk to you. I know he's troubled. . . . I sensed he wanted to, but . . ."

"We understand," Peterson said. "Can I leave you my card? It's a Chicago number, but should anything come up, you can reverse the charges."

As Mrs. Hervey was taking the card, I said, "Could I impose, and use your rest room for a moment?"

"Certainly," she said. She pointed. "It's down the hall, through Alex's study."

I moved quickly through the study, shutting the door behind me, went into the bathroom, turned the water on in the sink, and made rather a show of closing the bathroom door loudly. Then like a laser beam, I made for the book-and-paper-cluttered desk. I was frantically going through the papers, finding nothing but bills, when I noticed voices coming softly from a small, plastic, desktop intercom unit.

Peterson's voice, and Mrs. Hervey's! Apparently there was a two-way speaker by the front door, and the study intercom had been left on, only turned down.

Eavesdropping is one of the greatest tools a reporter has at his disposal.

So I turned it up.

"Perhaps we should wait for Mr. Brackett," Mrs. Hervey was saying.

"Mr. Brackett and I are collaborators," Peterson said. "You can go right ahead—there are no secrets between us."

I felt a momentary pang of disappointment, even betrayal, but then I smiled and thought, *No secrets as long as this little intercom is on*. . . .

"As I was saying, I really don't know what it is, but I found it here in this book Alex is reading. Or I should say that I've been sitting here, reading to Alex."

Not the front door—they had moved back to the bedroom. That made sense: She would have the intercoms throughout the house set up so that she could hear her husband call for her, wherever she might be.

"It's a computer disk," Mrs. Hervey was saying, "but I'm afraid I don't know anything about such things."

"I would think a scientist like your husband would have a lot of computer disks around," Peterson said.

"Not Alex. He never brought his work home with him. Not in thirty years. We don't even have a personal computer here at home. This disk, it says 'Beekman File' on it—would you like it?"

"Yes! Thank you, Mrs. Hervey. This could just the break I . . . break we've been looking for."

That was the end of their conversation. In the bathroom, I turned off the running water, and soon I was at the front door, where Peterson and Mrs. Hervey were waiting. Peterson seemed just a little nervous.

"Thank you, Mrs. Hervey," I said. "You've been very kind."

"Thank you for your concern," she said, and opened the door for us, then silently shut herself back inside with her dying husband.

We were walking back down the path. The pleasant breeze had turned chilly.

"She have anything interesting to say," I asked, "while I was in the john?"

"Not really," Peterson said. "It's just awful rough on her, seeing somebody she loves deteriorate like that."

"I know the feeling."

She gave me a quick look. "What?"

"Nothing."

In the car, she shrugged and said, "It was worth a try."

"But just another dead end, huh?"

"Another dead end," she confirmed.

"Well, we have a problem."

She gave me a pointed look. "Oh?"

"The bad guys think we have something we don't have. There's only one way to possibly survive this. We file columns telling our readers we're at a dead end. That we're moving on to new subjects—like a typical evening at Second City, or what it's like to experience 'funny hat' night at Comiskey Park, firsthand."

"Are you serious?"

I nodded. "Dead serious. We have to try to convince the bad guys we don't have what they want. That if we had it, we'd either turn it over to the cops, or splash it all over the papers."

"Are you saying this is the end of the story?"

"At least for right now. We need to spend a few low-key days, at least pretending it's over."

Her expression turned thoughtful. "Well . . . maybe you're right."

"Let's face it. We're up to rule number ten."

"Rule number ten?"

"It's what you do when all your leads dry up." I started the car.

"What's that?" she asked.

Joe Friday couldn't have delivered it any better.

"Go home," I said.

21

Red-eye

—

BYLINE: Sabrina Peterson

We didn't spend the night at the Honeymoon Hotel after all. Brackett managed, through the *Chronicle,* to get us a red-eye flight back to Chicago. And this time, my "husband" was extremely relieved to learn, first-class seats were available.

I came back from the rest room, trying not to show my frustration. Having gone to the trouble of lifting his wallet again, the least he could have done was leave that Chess Chemical security pass tucked in there. Where he was carrying it now, I had no idea.

He didn't think I saw him, his toe nudging my carryon back under the seat in front of mine. A couple of liars, that's what we were. I was halfway in, about to take my seat, when the plane lurched, hitting a pocket of turbulence, and I fell across his lap.

"Sorry," I said.

"No need to be."

We smiled at each other. It was a little forced.

At least the exercise had given me the opportunity to drop his wallet onto his seat alongside him.

Suddenly we had company. A flight attendant—a pleasant-looking woman well into her thirties, who had obviously been flying the friendly skies a good long time—loomed over us with a champagne bottle and two glasses.

"Champagne?" she asked cheerily.

Life in first class, I thought.

"Please," Brackett said, and I nodded, too.

"There you go, Mrs. Brackett. Mr. Brackett. Do you mind my asking . . . you wouldn't happen to be *newlyweds*, would you?"

I winced.

Brackett twitched a smile, and said, "Well, actually—yeah."

The flight attendant's smile was romantic. "You know, I can always spot the newlyweds on our Vegas flights. Congratulations, you two."

She went away, leaving the champagne bottle behind.

I looked at him sharply. "You booked us as Mr. and Mrs. Brackett?"

"*I* didn't book us. Jeannie, my secretary, did. Probably her idea of a joke."

"Oh. So the *Chronicle* knows all about it. Am I going to be in your column tomorrow? A description of me in a terrycloth robe?"

He raised his glass. "Lighten up, Mrs. Brackett.

I checked with Jeannie about our annulment, re-member? That's how and why she knew."

"Oh."

"I'll, uh, call you tomorrow afternoon, after you've had a chance to catch some rest . . . and we'll, you know—take care of that."

"Okay." I raised my champagne glass to his. "What shall we drink to?"

He gave me his rumpled smile. "To our annul-ment," he said, and raised his glass.

"To our annulment," I said, and we touched lips—the lips of our champagne glasses, that is.

He settled back in his seat. He had an expression that I could only describe as sentimental. "Frankly, Peterson, in all honesty . . . there's not another woman in the world I'd rather almost be married to."

I felt my eyes tearing up, and it enraged me. I tried not to show it.

"In all honesty," I said, "I don't think I could ever believe anything you said that included the phrase, 'in all honesty.'"

Now his expression seemed melancholy. "I can't blame you. I guess we're . . . two of a kind, aren't we?"

He was right. I was as bad as he was.

"Two of a kind," I said, and we clinked cham-pagne glasses again.

He was gazing at me with those beady little blue eyes—how could beady little blue eyes be so goddamned attractive?

He said, "Just because you cheat and lie and steal, that doesn't mean I hold it against you."

"Is that right? Strictly business, you mean?"

He swallowed. Were *his* eyes tearing up, too? "It doesn't mean I don't think of you very fondly."

I swallowed. "It doesn't mean I don't think fondly of you, either."

We settled back in our seats and sipped our champagne. I glanced down at my wedding band—my cheap, little gold-plated wedding band.

"Maybe it's time we took these off," I said, holding up my hand as I started to pull the ring off.

"Yeah," Brackett said, "you're probably right. The *Globe* marries the *Chronicle*—we wouldn't want that getting around."

His came off easily. Mine, embarrassingly, didn't. I tried to twist the damn thing off, but it wouldn't budge.

Brackett said, "You want some help with that?"

"Please."

"Don't take this wrong, now . . ."

And he took my hand and kissed me around my ring finger, and then he eased it off.

"You taste better than the ring," he said with a grin.

He hadn't let go of my hand yet.

His voice was a whisper. "Mrs. Brackett?"

"Yes, Mr. Brackett?"

"Just for old time's sake . . . would you mind . . . a small favor?"

"Anything," I said.

"How about giving your husband one last kiss?"

I touched his face and kissed him, a sweet, tender kiss that I would remember for a long time.

Then we settled back in our seats and didn't say anything else until the plane landed at O'Hare.

My editor, Rick Medwick, met me as I exited the security area, carryon slung over one shoulder, purse over the other. He looked pretty good for the middle of the night, though his thinning dark hair had a cowlick from his pillow that he hadn't had the time or maybe the energy to brush out.

"You don't look bad, considering," he said, helping me with my carryon as we stepped onto the escalator.

"You get those Yale yearbooks?"

"You bet."

"And?"

His half-smile didn't speak of success. "And your Ernesto Vargas wasn't in any of 'em. Have you got the Beekman disk?"

I patted the front pocket of my slacks. "Right here."

"I'm surprised Brackett didn't try to lift it."

"He did. He thinks he has it right now."

Glancing to my left, at the stairs adjacent to the escalator, I saw Brackett jogging down them, talking intensely with his editor, Matt Greenfield. Brackett's eyes met mine, and he gave me a tiny smile and a little salute.

"Peterson," he said.

"Brackett," I said, nodding, returning the salute.

Then they were gone, and Rick was asking, "Why does he think he has the Beekman disk?"

"Because he stole a disk labeled 'Beekman file' from my carry-on bag, on the plane."

Rick grinned. "What's on it?"

"My phone list. I always carry that, with my laptop."

He was laughing as we reached the bottom. "Sneaky girl. I like that about you. You gonna take a little time and catch some rest?"

"That depends."

"On what?"

"On when the next flight back to Spring Creek, Wisconsin, is."

My editor sighed and smiled, shaking his head. His expression was admiring. "Gotta hand it to you, kid. You're one aggressive reporter."

For some reason, I felt like he'd slapped me, not complimented me. "Thanks," I said numbly.

"But if we book you a flight, you gotta promise me one thing."

"Yeah?"

"You'll catch some sleep on the plane. You look like you haven't slept in days. Your eyes are all red."

"Really?" I said.

And we went looking for my new plane ticket. In coach.

22

Round Trip

—

BYLINE: Peter Brackett

I woke up Monday morning, wondering what the hell happened to Sunday.

But it was definitely Monday. At least when I clicked on the TV, that seemed to be Bryant Gumbel's opinion. This was what I got for not sleeping for two or three days. My answering-machine light was blinking at me furiously. I let it blink.

Rising like the Mummy, I fixed myself some microwave breakfast, and read the *Chronicle* that had been delivered to my front door—where my column usually was were the words "Peter Brackett is on assignment."

Then I shaved, showered, and made myself more or less presentable. Back in my bedroom, I removed the Beekman computer disk from where I'd masking-taped it under my night table. And I spilled out Kim's Chess Chemical security badge from a Crackerjacks box onto the coffee table in the living room.

Time to get to work.

But when I tried the Beekman disk in the computer, and saw the words SABRINA PETERSON— REVISED PHONE LIST appear on the screen, I had a sinking feeling.

Then when I called the *Globe* and was told that Ms. Peterson was out of the office, the sinking feeling sank further. When would Ms. Peterson be back? They didn't know—seemed Ms. Peterson was "on assignment."

You know—like Peter Brackett supposedly was.

Out of desperation, I tried her apartment, and got only her friendly sounding voice requesting that I leave a message.

Somehow I resisted the urge to do so.

By the following morning, a clear sunny wonder of a morning at that, I was entering the black tower of Chess Chemical's corporate headquarters in scenic Spring Creek, Wisconsin. You remember Spring Creek, don't you? Pastoral home of cows, single girls, Boy Scouts, hired assassins, and LDF?

"Good morning," I said to the receptionist, the same blazer-wearing brunette I'd seen there before. But she didn't seem to recognize me, either from my previous visit or from my appearances on *Letterman* and *Today*. Maybe my sunglasses were presenting an impenetrable disguise.

Anyway, I inquired about the next available tour, and she pleasantly pointed to a group of tourists that was just queuing up.

I slipped my sunglasses in my sport's coat pocket; the security badge was in there, too. Staying in back, I watched out for Kim or anyone else who might recognize me. The tour guide was going through the usual spiel.

"Good morning, everyone, and welcome to Chess Chemical," the young woman was saying. "Our first stop this morning will be the Life Sciences building."

The voice seemed familiar.

I moved forward, easing through the crowd, getting a few dirty looks, but all I could see was the back of the tour guide's Polyvon Plus uniform. She was a brunette. I willed her to turn around.

She did.

"As we move down the 'Biology of Tomorrow' corridor," Sabrina Peterson said, smiling wide, gesturing gracefully, "I'd like to point out that you're walking on a space-age, stain-resistant carpet and surrounded by shatterproof windows, both created here at Chess."

My poleaxed expression no doubt reflected the thought pulsing through what was left of my brain: *How the hell had she managed this since Saturday night?*

But perfect little tour guide that she was, the brunette-bewigged, bespectacled Peterson didn't flinch upon seeing my astonished face. Not a thing registered on her pretty countenance. Not even the smug sense of superiority that must have been coursing through her, under the Polyvon Plus.

Regaining my composure, I did my best to blend in among the crowd of kids and parents and couples, and when Peterson took them inside the IMAX Surround-Sound theater for the thrilling presentation, *New Horizons for Chess,* I stayed in the hall, lying in wait.

Pretty soon she came out for a drink of water at the fountain—at least, that was her game. She knew I was out there.

Still bending over the drinking fountain, she said in her cheery guide voice, "You're missing the show, sir."

"I don't think so."

"You look familiar. Aren't you somebody famous?"

"Yeah. I'm the 'Sucker of the Year.' Didn't you see the cover of *Time*?"

"Missed that one." She stood and faced me, arms folded, openly smug now.

Trying to sound hurt, I said, "I can't believe you double-crossed me like this. This is supposed to be *our* story."

Her face hardened. "Is that why you lifted Kim's security pass without telling me?"

"I was going to tell you."

"When and where? In your column? By the way, when you get a chance, drop my phone list in the mail to me, would you?"

"We're partners, Peterson. This is dangerous. You need me."

"No. You see, I have my own security pass now. And the one you have? It won't work—once an employee reports his or her pass missing, as Kim no doubt has by now, the code is changed."

"How did you manage . . ."

Her shrug was casual, but her smile was triumphant. "I may have never mentioned it to you, Brackett, but I'm blessed with a near-photographic memory. I paid attention on the tour, plus I knew they were short a tour guide here. When I applied yesterday, I rattled off the entire tour guide spiel . . . and what do you know? I got the job."

"This is dangerous. What if Kim or her friend Darlene sees you? What if *Willy Chess* sees you?"

She raised her chin, defensive. "I'm being careful. The wig, the glasses . . ."

"Are you kidding? It's not safe for you to be here. Let's do this together, some *other* way."

"No."

"What happened to our vows? Till death do us part?"

Her smirk was withering. "You're reaching. Brackett, the game is over. I've got a security pass, and I've got the real Beekman disk. You've got bupkis. Now, do you leave quietly, or do I use the authority vested in me as a Chess Chemical employee to get you thrown out on your lying ass?"

"You wouldn't do that," I said. "Not after all we've been through. . . ."

At least they didn't literally throw me on what *I* like to think of as my prize-winning, celebrity ass; but the two armed guards in Polyvon Plus jumpsuits were certainly efficient in doing their duty as Chess Chemical employees.

And I'd made a round trip to the Chess Chemical parking lot in record time—I didn't even get to finish the damn tour.

I spoke to Sam Smotherman from my room at the Mill Creek Inn, where I was tossing my things in my carryon.

"I appreciate your efforts, Sam," I said, cradling the phone with my neck, "but you might as well forget it."

"I can keep trying," Sam said. "But I keep drawing a blank on this Vargas. I've talked to the alumni association, the registrar's office, even some old friends."

"Forget it. It's not my story anymore."

"You're not on the story?"

"Nope. It's all hers. She can have it."

"Sabrina Peterson, you mean."

"Yeah," I said, zipping the carryon. I sat on the edge of the bed, phone still cradled. "Crazy broad. You know what she did? Got herself a job as a damn Chess tour guide!"

"You gotta be kidding."

"I wish I were. I'm afraid she's in over her head."

He grunted. "Well, if I find something out about Vargas, do you want me to get in touch with *her*?"

"I don't give a damn, Sam. Really I don't. I'm just not interested anymore."

"Okay. Hey, I'm gonna be in Chicago next week. You want to meet at the Berghoff for lunch, say, Tuesday?"

"No can do, Sam. I had the *Chronicle* make a connection to Seattle for me."

"What's in Seattle?"

"The tattered remnants of my novel-writing career: the first leg on the revised schedule of my book tour."

He chuckled at that. "Hey, well, give 'em hell."

"Gotta go, Sam. Thanks for your efforts, pal."

An hour later, I was in my seat on Flight 167 to Seattle. I was in first class, of course, and had taken early boarding, and other passengers were still filing onto the jet. I sat sipping a Coke, wondering why the attractive, redheaded flight attendant, who'd been so complimentary about *White Lies*, had failed to stir certain impulses within me that were invariably stirred by the likes of a redheaded flight attendant.

That damn Peterson was on my mind. I was worried about her. Couldn't help myself. Then I thought about my having mentioned to Sam that she'd taken that Chess Chemical tour guide job. If Sam didn't understand she'd gone undercover, if he tried to get ahold of her—should some Ernesto Vargas information belatedly turn up—he could possibly blow her cover.

I figured I'd better call Sam from Seattle and warn him not to try to contact Peterson directly, and then I started thinking about the attempts on our lives, and particularly the thin assassin, and I got very nervous.

It was an ominous feeling I just couldn't shake.

"Is there a phone on the plane?" I asked the redhead.

By now the plane was fully boarded, and we were on the runway, waiting for our turn. The captain had already apologized for the delay, assuring us we were next in line for takeoff.

She bent over me; her Chanel Number 5 only served to remind me of the woman who was still legally my wife. Pointing, she said, "The phone is straight ahead on the cabin wall—but you really should stay seated, sir. You can call from the air."

"All right," I said.

But when her back was to me, I unsnapped my seat belt and went forward for the phone. It was a portable that operated off your credit card. I took it back to my seat, then dug in my pocket for that business card with Sam's direct line on it.

But the card just wasn't there. The now useless Chess Chemical security badge was there, but I'd apparently left the card with the number I needed by the phone on the nightstand at the Mill Creek Inn.

Muttering obscenities, I tried information. "Madison, please—the state capitol building."

To hear the number, I had to cover my other ear to muffle the captain's announcement that the flight attendants should prepare for departure.

Then I called the state capitol, and asked for Sam Smotherman.

"That's extension 307," the operator said. "I'll connect you—"

But I'd already clicked off, having already made a more important connection.

Sam Smotherman was extension number 307.

Sam Smotherman was extension number 307 as written on the slip of paper in the parka pocket of a man who'd been sent to kill Peterson and me.

Sam Smotherman was extension number 307 as written on the envelope in the wastebasket of the murdered Darryl Beekman, Jr.

Sam Smotherman was extension number 307 whom I'd told, a little more than hour before, that Sabrina Peterson was working undercover at Chess Chemical.

I was in the aisle.

The redheaded flight attendant, who earlier had found me so attractive, was reassessing her opinion.

"Sir!" she said, her eyes wide and startled. "You simply must take your seat—we're about to take off!"

"Stop the plane."

Her smile was both incredulous and a little frightened. "Sir, I'm afraid at this point, we can't—"

"Stop the fucking plane or I'm jumping out."

"Sir, you'll have . . ."

I brushed her aside—didn't shove her, exactly—

but soon I had my hands on the emergency exit, ready to pull.

"Tell the pilot," I told her, as she came up, white with shock, "it's a matter of life and death."

"All right, all right! We'll stop the plane."

She went into the cockpit and I was still at the emergency exit when the jet screeched to a stop.

She came back to reassure me, but I could tell something was up.

I looked at her hard. "They've called the cops, haven't they?"

"Sir . . ."

"You know who I am. I'm a reporter. I'm not a nut, or skyjacker. I don't want to take this plane to Cuba, I just want *off*—to save a life! Understand? Do you want a life on *your* conscience?"

She was thinking; her eyes were flickering behind narrow slits. "What is it?" she whispered. "Are you investigating a story about the Mafia or something?"

"Yes! Yes! It's a Mafia hit, and only you and I can stop it."

She smiled. Nodded. Then whispered, "I can let the emergency ladder down, and maybe you can beat the police here."

She did, and I did. The airport security car was gliding up as I slipped away, skirting around the runway and heading back into the airport. Soon I was out front, looking futilely for a cab.

A woman of about fifty in a fur stole and a black dress was arguing with her husband. He was a heavy-set man in a baggy suit, and was a little older than she was, unloading luggage from the trunk of their rental Ford. Their accents were pure New York.

"Howard, if you insist on taking this vehicle back

to Hertz, you will *not* make the flight. I swear, I'll take it *with*-out you!"

Before Howard could take her up on it, I stepped up and said, "Hertz curb service."

And I held out my hand.

Howard smiled a little. "Something new."

"Just 'cause we're not number two," I said with a big smile, "that doesn't mean we don't try harder."

That sounded good to Howard, and he gave me the car keys, putting his wife immediately into a better mood.

"What a nice young man," she said. "And what a lovely airport!"

Howard, holding out a dollar tip, followed me as I was hopping behind the wheel.

"You've done enough," I said, and smiled and waved, and threw the car in gear. The way I laid rubber, Howard and the missus must have figured Hertz needed that car back in a New York minute.

23

Band of Gold

—

BYLINE: Sabrina Peterson

The Biology of Tomorrow corridor, where I'd guided five groups of tourists here at my first day at Chess Chemical, was dimly lit after the close of business. For a long two hours, I had hidden in a stall in the employee locker room, after having a couple close calls with Kim. Other than Willy Chess himself, she was the only one I was worried might see past my glasses and brown hair.

Maybe I should have left the tour guide uniform on, but the Polyvon Plus made my skin itch. I got into my sweater and slacks, and with my purse slung over my shoulder, went out to do some serious snooping.

I was nearing the LDF Research Farm entrance—the one that had sirens blaring and signals flashing when that little boy touched it the other day—hoping the Chess security pass clutched in my hot little hand would bypass all that fuss.

Maybe it wouldn't.

After all, I didn't know of any security check that had been run on me—my fake I.D., courtesy of the *Globe*, had been accepted unquestioningly by a personnel man dazzled by my smile and mastery of the tour guide gospel. But maybe Kim's badge was a higher-priority one—maybe a *new*, lower-priority employee's badge would *set off* the alarms.

On the other hand, I'd seen a tour guide shut the alarms off with her badge, hadn't I? So what was I worrying about?

I was contemplating all of this, badge in hand, when I heard footsteps padding slowly down the space-age, stain-resistant carpet.

I ducked into the ladies' room.

Peeking out a few moments later, I saw one of the armed, uniformed security guards rounding the far end of the corridor. He would have walked right past me.

But he was gone now, and I crossed the hall and inserted the badge in the entry panel above the door latch. The panel lighted up, glowing reassuringly in the dim light of the corridor, and a *click* signaled the door unlocking.

I went in.

And found myself in a narrow, stainless-steel corridor. My frightened reflection bounced off the walls at me a thousand times, and I clutched myself. It was cold. Icy cold.

Also, quiet.

Deathly quiet, until it was broken by the cavernous echoing of my feet on the stainless-steel floor. Where was that synthetic-fiber carpeting when I could use it?

At the end of the reflecting hallway was a metal door. Again, my reflection looked back at me, and seemed to be asking me what the hell I thought I was doing, opening this door like that.

And then I was inside the LDF research farm.

Only it was more like a prison than a farm. I was in a carpeted, central observation and work area—desks and workstations and laboratory tables— looking up three stories at a greenhouse-style roof. Balconies with catwalks bordered stainless-steel cell blocks where various animals were caged. On those cells glowed gauges of blue, green, and orange, monitoring vital signs, apparently. The lighting was subdued, the entire chamber cast in a soft eerie blue. Air was circulating. The ventilation system was obviously state-of-the-art, although doing little to tone down the zoolike odor.

Here and there, among the laboratory trappings of the ground-floor observation area of the huge room, were computer stations. I was settling in at the nearest one when a whir made me look up and notice a security camera above, making a slow scan of the room.

And I was in its path.

I backed up against the cell behind me, its stainless-steel bars cold against my neck. This put me out of the camera's eye, but I almost jumped into its view when something nudged me.

Startled, I looked back and saw a small cow, its eyes gazing tragically up at me.

"Moo," it said, but only half-heartedly.

The camera had missed me, and moving along its

robotic track, was starting over on its circuit of the facility. That would give me a few minutes at least.

I scurried to the nearest computer, booted it up and inserted the Beekman file disk Mrs. Hervey had given me.

The machine was an Apple, and I was used to an IBM. It took me a while to get the thing up and running. And I had to shut it down, once, when the camera made its circuit again. Took about four minutes, I noted.

So I went back to keep my friend the cow company for a while. Then when the camera wasn't looking, I tried the computer again.

"DECODING IN PROGRESS—PLEASE WAIT," its screen said.

Please wait—but how *long*? The camera was making its inexorable swing. . . .

I sat blinking at the green screen, and then it blinked at me and said, "DECODING PROCESS COMPLETED. PRESS ANY KEY TO CONTINUE."

"All right," I whispered to myself, and pushed a key, any old key, and the screen spoke to me again.

"DARRYL BEEKMAN'S CHRISTMAS LIST," it said.

Mouth agape, I began scrolling through perhaps a hundred names and addresses.

"Shit," I said.

There was a *click* and I looked up. The surveillance cam had stopped. *What did that mean?*

I looked behind me.

Nothing.

I swallowed, and turned back to the computer screen. The list of names and addresses stared back at me. After all this, just another dead end—

"You could always view it as a list of leads," someone said.

With a gasp, I turned and saw the shape of a man in the shadows by the cages. Cows began to moo, and the bray of sheep and goats made a strange overture as the shape emerged into the blue light.

He was a small man with dark curly hair and a ready smile, and he called himself Sam Smotherman.

"A very, very nice try. A first-rate effort." He was shaking his head, smiling a little, his expression admiring. "You really are a remarkable investigative journalist, Ms. Peterson. Or after your recent episode in Las Vegas, perhaps I should call you 'Mrs. Brackett?'"

"Perhaps I should call you 'Mr. Vargas?'" I said. "Or do you prefer 'Ernesto?'"

His eyes widened in surprise, and the smile disappeared, but just for a moment. He was all teeth when he said, "*Muy bien*. And how did you make this discovery? I took considerable care covering my tracks."

I shrugged. "When I asked you what year you graduated, you were vague . . . gave me two years. That struck me as little unusual, so I started looking at yearbooks, beginning with the two years you'd mentioned."

"Didn't find me, did you?"

"No. Not for a while. And not under 'Smotherman.'"

Another shape moved in the darkness, stepping out into the blue light: a tall thin man with a cadaverous face and a distinctive khaki suit.

And a big gun in his hand. A revolver—the kind you see in Dirty Harry movies.

"Mando's an admirer of yours," Smotherman said. His smile was teasing as he gestured toward the thin man with the big gun. "He's been following you everywhere."

I was just thinking that I didn't like knowing Mando's name when I heard footsteps on the catwalk above. Glancing up, I saw another familiar face, frowning down at me.

Willy Chess.

"Ms. Peterson," he said, his voice echoing off the metal bars and walls, "I've had excellent reports on your performance here at Chess Chemical today. But you unfortunately seem to have made several deceptive statements on your application."

"You can't fire me," I said, trembling but trying to not show it, "I quit."

"We were hoping," Willy said, coming down a metal stairway, "that you had what we were looking for. But since you apparently don't, we can safely assume it didn't survive the crash."

"You mean the duplicate copy of the Beekman test results?" I said. "Maybe I *do* have it."

"No," Smotherman said, coldly, his glad-handing mask dropped completely now, "you're *looking* for it." And he waved a dismissive hand toward the computer and the Beekman Christmas list displayed there.

"You're *sure* about that?" I said, still trying to run the bluff. "You're not really going to be safe until *all* the evidence is destroyed."

"You're right," Smotherman said, gesturing to his friend Mando, who moved up beside him. "But the only evidence left to destroy is . . . you."

"What about Brackett?" Willy said. For all his talk, he seemed at least as nervous as I did.

"Brackett, too," Smotherman said. "But he'll be no problem. He trusts me, and I know right where he is . . . Seattle, on his book tour."

A door opened, startling all of us. I half expected Brackett to step in, and prove Smotherman wrong. Mando slipped behind me, putting the big gun in the small of my back. All of our eyes were large as the young security guard stepped into view.

And my heart sank.

"Oh!" he said. "Mr. Chess—I didn't know anybody was in here."

Willy stepped forward. "What's going on, Ted?"

The guard wasn't in on it!

But my cadaverous-faced chaperon shoved the gun harder against my spine, ending any thought I might have had about alerting the young man.

"Somebody shut off the security camera in here," the guard was saying. "I was just checking it out."

"I did that," Willy said. "My friends and I needed a little privacy. Understood?"

"Sure," the guard said, though he was obviously wondering what exactly our little party was about. "But you should be aware, Mr. Chess, that we're investigating a possible security breach."

Willy frowned. "What do you mean?"

"Probably nothing. But there was some sort of disturbance out by the loading dock."

Willy looked at Smotherman, who narrowed his eyes and nodded.

"I'll go with you," Willy told the security guard. "We'll check it out together."

Smotherman spoke softly in Spanish, looking toward me as if I understood, which I did not. But the final word he said was "Mando."

He'd been giving directions to my cadaverous "admirer," who stepped out from behind me, having slipped his weapon away somewhere, following Willy and the security guard out a side exit.

That left just Smotherman and me, and I was looking for something to toss at him when he said, "Don't bother."

He was facing me with a small gun in his hand. Not Dirty Harry-size, just a little revolver, but I had a feeling it could do the job.

"I'm surprised Willy got you involved in this, Sam," I said. "I know you go way back and all, but I mean, after the way you screwed up that fire back in college."

"I've improved with age, Ms. Peterson. Something you won't get the chance to do, I'm afraid."

"But Willy didn't come to you for murder and cover-up, did he? Not at first. Initially, it was for you to get next to Senator Robbins. How are you going get her to approve LDF, anyway? She doesn't strike me as the type you can buy off."

"We won't have to," he said smugly. "She trusts me."

I shook my head. "Why did you risk it, after all these years? You obviously went to a great deal of trouble and expense to establish a new identity, and you've been very successful at your lobbying and politicking."

With his free hand he elaborately gestured to himself. "Ms. Peterson, with the money involved here, yet *another* 'me' can emerge from the ashes of Sam Smotherman—just as he arose from the ashes of Ernesto Vargas."

"How poetic."

"What's keeping them?" he said to himself, irritably. Then he added, "Don't move," and cocking the revolver, went to the side exit where Willy, Mando, and the security guard had gone out.

I was looking for something to use as a weapon,

but then Willy and Mando appeared at the doorway, where they spoke in hushed tones to Smotherman. I thought I made out the word "Rats," but whether it was an expression of displeasure of just a description of another lab animal, I had no idea.

They were crossing over to me when Willy noticed something on the carpet, picked it up, shrugged, and tossed it absentmindedly in the air, as if it were a coin.

It looked like a ring.

"We've got a little traffic jam problem outside," Smotherman said.

"Hey, I'm in no hurry," I said.

Willy was getting nervous. He began to pace, and got tired of the game of tossing the ring he'd found up and down.

He pitched it over on the counter by the computer, near me, and it made a little metallic pinging song, dancing side to side, as it settled to a stop. I glanced at it.

It was a wedding ring.

The cheap gold-plated band of a wedding ring.

24

Health Hazard

BYLINE: Peter Brackett

I left my "borrowed" rental car along the roadside and, for the last half mile, made my approach to Chess Chemical on foot. The chemical company complex stood out in the night, haloed by more lights than a night game at Wrigley Field. The satellite sheds of the research farms fanned out from the black central shaft like outstretched tentacles; the partially built Life Sciences Building, with its beams showing, loomed like a colossal robot in the background.

The entire network of buildings was protected by a high, electric fence.

I approached the rear-entry guard shack, keeping

down low, having no idea in hell how I was going to get in there.

And get in there I must: Peterson was inside. I knew she was. It was where I would've been.

Maybe if there was only one guard in that shack, I could overpower him. I'm not small. I'm not exactly weak. I was building my confidence up for the attempt when I got close enough to see *two* armed sentries at the guard station.

And I began feeling very small, and very weak, indeed.

Still in a crouch, moving along the narrow access road toward the shack, I heard a rumbling behind me, glanced over my shoulder, and saw headlights bearing down.

I dove for the ditch, hoping I hadn't been seen, and an unmarked delivery truck came barreling by.

What the hell: I hopped up onto the skid ramp in back, bracing myself by holding on to the latch of its corrugated pull-down door. Then I used one of the two logical options you have with a pull-down door: I pulled up on it.

It was not locked, thank God, and I raised the door up just far enough for me to slide inside, and closed it behind me just as the vehicle was stopping at the guard shack.

Something smelled, and not in the figurative sense. Something was making noises, chittering sort of sounds, and I felt something touching my cheek, and pulled away. Digging in my sports jacket pockets, I found my matchbook and used my last remaining match, striking it to see just what the hell, or *who* the hell, I had hitched a ride with.

Stacked floor to ceiling were cages. In those cages were all of the rats in the world.

Maybe not all. But close. Close to every goddamn beady redeyed one of them. Staring back at me, indignantly.

They chattered and chittered and showed me their teeth and I blew out the match.

No wonder somebody hadn't bothered locking the damn truck.

I was huddled against the corrugated door, numb with unjustifiable but nonetheless incontestable fright, when the truck's brakes squealed, further exciting my fellow passengers. The vehicle jarred to a halt.

Peeking out a slat in the side of the truck, I could see two things: We had pulled up to a loading dock at the rear of the black spire of Chess Chemical; and a sign up by the garage doors of the dock that said: RESEARCH FARM - SECURITY CLEARANCE REQUIRED.

Then I saw something else: two whitesuited workers, standing up on the loading dock, snugging on work gloves. The kind of work gloves you might snug on if you had to deal with cages full of rats.

Then the truck was backing up, toward the loading dock.

I looked into the darkness, listened to the rats chittering, and whispered, "Good idea," to them.

When the two workers pulled the corrugated door up, five thousand (give or take a hundred or two) rats came squealing out of there, all but flying as if the Pied Piper were playing one hell of a tune. They were frantic, squealing—and I'm referring not only to the rats, but to the two workers and a truck driver and a security guard who'd been behind the vehicle when the sea of rats came swarming out and over them.

The rats ran in all directions and so, at least for the moment, did the humans present, all but one. Head covered by my jacket, I plowed through the rodent exodus and made my way through the emptying cages to the cabin of the truck and slipped out the driver's door.

Then I danced through the rats—possibly squishing one or two, but don't tell the Humane Society— and smiled as I saw only the backs of the fleeing security guard, truck driver, and workers. I leaped up onto the loading dock and went inside. Beyond the loading area, I found a thick metal door with a small rectangular window. I peeked in.

And I had found her.

Peterson.

But so had someone else: Sam Smotherman.

And just as I was muttering "Shit" to myself, I saw that skinny, cadaverous-pussed, son of a bitch slip out of the shadows behind Smotherman, and into the dim blue light of the cavernous laboratory where this unfortunate confrontation was taking place.

The thin man had a gun in his hand, pointing it at Peterson—a .44 Magnum. The most powerful handgun in the world, as somebody once said.

The metal door was locked.

I looked around the loading area desperately, knowing I'd have company soon and needed to get out of there, in any case, and spotted metal fire-escape stairs leading to a landing and another door.

On the landing, another window gave me a view of what appeared to be a very calm Peterson chatting with Smotherman.

But this door was locked as well.

Another fire-escape landing was to my left, perhaps twenty-five feet away. But there was no easy way to get to it. In fact, the only way I could think of was to grab on to a dangling cargo rope just within my reach, and play fucking Tarzan.

Which is what I did, balancing in a singularly ungainly fashion on the railing of the landing, and swinging across the other landing.

That was the plan.

Instead, I wound up dangling by the damn thing, thirty feet in the air.

Looking down, I saw only cement. Looking up, there was another landing, where hay bales were stacked. I explored my options. Weeping seemed the best one. But nonetheless, I struggled like the fattest kid in gym class as I climbed the rope, panting, hands burning, and summoning one final burst of energy, thrusting myself over a railing and onto the landing, where I promptly made myself at home among a family of goats. They started grunting at me, but I raised my finger to my lips and went *shush*.

And I'll be damned if they didn't quiet down.

I got to my feet. My lower back couldn't have hurt more; my hands were red and raw from the rope. By the way, where the hell was I?

This was, apparently, the third-floor landing of the research farm. Carefully, quietly, I let myself out of the cage of goats and moved along the metal-mesh floor, peeking over the railing.

Smotherman was keeping Peterson covered as he walked to a side door and spoke with a harried-looking Willy Chess and the skinny hit man, whose name seemed to be Mando.

I heard them mention "rats," so the problem in the loading dock area had been reported, apparently.

Moving carefully, I edged around until I was almost directly over Peterson. I needed to signal her, but I dared not speak. Too many men, too many guns. I had to think this through, but I wanted her to know the cavalry, understaffed though it might be, had arrived. Searching my pockets, I stumbled onto the wedding band.

Perfect.

I moved cautiously to the edge of the balcony and tossed the ring down—didn't dare shoot for the metallic counter next to her. I was aiming for the floor near her feet.

But I overshot a little, and she didn't notice it fall—her eyes were searching the desk, probably looking for a makeshift weapon there.

Damn, I thought.

Then Willy Chess noticed the ring, and I moved back into the darkness, back against a cage with more goats in it. They were making some noise, but so were a lot of the other animals in this three-story combination madhouse-and-zoo.

"Hey," Peterson was saying down there, "I'm in no hurry."

I edged carefully back to where I could see them. Willy was tossing the ring up and down, like he was George Raft flipping a silver dollar!

But then he got bored with it or nervous or something, and tossed the ring over on the counter by the computer, where it finally caught Peterson's attention.

I watched, sitting on proverbial pins and needles.

And then she stole a look up at me. Her elated expression lasted only an instant, before she removed it to maintain her prisoner-style composure. I looked toward Smotherman and the other two men. They were huddled together, talking, probably deciding the particulars of Peterson's fate.

When she stole another glance up at me, I mouthed, *Keep them talking,* and she nodded imperceptibly, and I faded back. What could I do? Throw a goat at 'em? Hell.

Looking around frantically, I spotted a fuse box on the wall at the far end of the landing. Usually a reporter threw light on a subject; this time, the opposite might make more sense. . . .

Down below, Peterson was doing as I asked.

"As long as you guys got some time to kill," she was saying, "Why don't you at least satisfy my journalistic curiosity?"

"You want an *interview*?" Sam said, incredulous.

I walked slowly along the landing, toward the fuse box.

"Why not? What do you say, Willy? Level with me—why didn't you just cop to LDF being a flop?"

Then Willy Chess's strained voice replied: "I could have . . . if I'd only spent two or three million on it. Even five. Could've written it off, just so much research and development. But I had two scientists who were convinced they could iron out all the problems, if I would just keep pouring in the money. A hundred million later, there was no turning back."

I stopped. *Hey,* I thought. *This is good stuff.*

I dug in my pocket for my spiral pad. Couldn't find a pen, but there was a pencil at a counter by a little lab station near one of the goat cages. I started jotting down notes.

"But the scientists were wrong," Peterson said.

Willy's voice was falsely jovial. "Yes, and they were big about it—they admitted their mistake." Now even the mock gaiety was gone. "But it was too late—I'd mortgaged the company's future on LDF. It had to be a success. If my father found out how I'd bungled things . . ."

I kept writing, moving slowly toward the fuse box as I did.

"What did the *real* test results say, Willy?" she asked. "How bad *is* this shit?"

There was a long pause.

Then Willy's voice gave the answer: "Both Beekman and Hervey said there was a clear link to cancer."

And now my old pal Smotherman put in his two cents: "And you can't exactly stick a label on milk cartons warning use of the product may be hazardous to your health."

"Oh I don't know," Peterson said bitterly. "Why not? Half your market share on this product can't even read yet."

Willy's voice sounded regretful. He practically seemed near tears. "It's that goddamn Beekman's fault . . . I offered him a fortune, if he'd sign off on LDF."

"But Willy," Peterson said, "it was bound to show up. Even if you put the fix in at the FDA, and with Senator Robbins's committee, the cancer wouldn't stay hidden."

Smotherman said, "That's what bank accounts in Zurich are for, Ms. Peterson. Well—now you have your story. Pulitzer–Prize material, if you ask me . . . with one slight drawback: No one's ever going to read it."

Don't bet on it, asshole, I thought, slipping my notebook away.

I had my hand on the fuse box, and from here I could see a disturbing tableau: Sam nodded to

Mando, who yanked Peterson away from the computer station and toward the side door. The barrel of the .44 was against her head. Smotherman and Willy were heading for the front exit.

"Where are they *taking* me, Sam?" Peterson called, her eyes were stealing tiny looks up toward where I'd been.

I opened the fuse box, and said to myself, *Woops.*

"You work in Chicago," Smotherman said. "It's a time-honored tradition."

"What, another fire?"

A hundred fuses or more stared back at me with their dead glass eyes, and no sign of a master switch.

Smotherman said, "No - it's called being taken for a ride."

Peterson's voice down there sounded frenzied now. "Oh—another *train* ride, you mean?"

Each fuse was labeled —LIFE SUPPORT, ROW 1; LIFE SUPPORT, ROW 2—how I wished I taken that damn Eveyln Wood speed reading course.

Smotherman sounded as calm as he did smug. "I don't want to spoil the surprise for you. Besides, this interview is over . . . Mrs. Brackett."

Then he said something in Spanish to his friend Mando, and I heard a small, very ominous click, making a tiny echo across the steel chamber: the cocking of the .44

"*Peter!*" she screamed.

"Hit the deck, Sabrina!" I yelled, and unscrewed what I prayed was the fuse that would throw this room into darkness.

It was, but the room briefly illuminated in a flash of orange and blue as Mando fired his big gun.

25

Mightier than the Sword

BYLINE: Sabrina Peterson

The roar of the gun firing over my head was deafening, and its echoing from the steel surfaces of the room sent me scrambling across the carpet in the darkness, keeping low.

"Cover the exits!" Smotherman yelled.

I felt my way along, and soon realized I was next to a lab table. Reaching up, I could feel test tubes in a tray. I grabbed the thing and hurled it—it landed with a shatter that attracted reverberating gunfire. I found another test-tube tray, and repeated the process, drawing the gunfire to my left as I moved to the right.

My hands found the cold steel surface of a wall as I felt my way along. If I'd managed to keep my sense of direction in the hubbub (not to mention the dark), there should be a door along here.

And there was.

I opened it quickly, quietly, and slipped inside another dark room. The zoo smell was just as strong, if not stronger, and I could hear the panting and snorting of lab animals. I was glancing back at the darkness where I'd come from when a door opposite me opened, and I backed up against metal bars, startling whatever animal was caged behind them.

The door's opening had cast a small amount of light into the room—possibly from an adjacent room through whose windows leeched illumination from the security lighting outside.

And that light source, meager though it was, allowed me to make out the silhouette of a figure—a man—in the doorway.

I might have screamed or fought back, but the shadowy shape had seen me, too, and was on me so fast, I didn't know what hit me.

But something did hit me—a fist in the eye, rocking me back against the cage, rattling it, and me, as I slid to the floor in a pile.

I was surprised it hadn't put my lights out, but in fact, almost at that exact moment, the electricity clicked back on. And I could clearly see (from the eye I wasn't covering with a hand, that is) the man attached to the fist that had hit me.

"Peterson," Brackett whispered, aghast at what he'd done, leaning over with me with the fist turning into a helping hand, "I didn't know it was you."

"There are laws against wife beating, you know," I whispered back, holding my already swelling eye.

I tried to stand up, but stumbled, and he braced me.

"Couldn't stay away from a good story, huh?" I said softly.

"Couldn't stay away from a good woman," he said.

I hugged him and he was gently patting my back, when the sound of running footsteps snapped us back to reality.

"There's a stairwell," I whispered, pointing, and Brackett nodded, taking my hand. We went quickly but quietly up the metal stairs, me first, onto the first of the cell-block catwalks. We moved carefully along the railing, past a row of robotic arms that was performing routine monitoring functions on ranks of test tubes.

Then the sound of feet coming up those same metal stairs sent us crouching behind a lab counter, holding our breath.

Someone was approaching—his shoes creaked on the metal-mesh floor.

As we crouched down, Brackett looked up, his eyes narrowing in thought as he studied a robotic arm feeding test tubes above us.

The footsteps were getting nearer, and Brackett stood, grabbed the robotic arm, swinging it around and slamming it into the cadaverous face of our stalker, with enough force to knock him back into another counter, where assorted beakers, tubes, and vials shattered and splashed from the impact.

Then we were running, and Brackett pointed up ahead—an elevator! I slammed my fist on the Up button, and we waited, as behind us the thin man was slowly rising, like Frankenstein's creature, from the clutter of broken glass.

Despite the fall he'd taken—even despite a jagged, knifelike sliver embedded in his arm, his sleeve already soaked red with blood—Mando had managed to hold on to his Dirty Harry gun.

And he was aiming it right at us as the elevator doors opened. We jumped in, and as the steel doors closed, first one, then another bullet *whanged* against them.

Safely within the metal womb of the elevator, I reached my hand toward the buttons, finger poised at two, when Brackett grabbed my wrist.

"Wait a second," he whispered.

I gave him a puzzled look, but then he waited another moment, grinned, and hit the Door Open button, and we exited again. We heard Mando's footsteps as he clambered up to the next floor.

Then Brackett reached his hand in the elevator, pressed two, pulled his arm out, and sent the empty car up.

Now I got the picture.

Brackett, keeping down, went up the metal stairs, without a sound, to the second floor, and I followed him the same way.

We were behind the surprised Mando as he stood facing the elevator doors opening onto an empty car.

"Lose something?" Brackett asked.

And as Mando turned, Brackett drove a fist into the man's groin, knocking him backward, howling in pain. Best of all, his hand popped open, sending the .44 clattering along the metal-mesh floor. Brackett dove for the gun, but Mando—despite his bloody arm and the low blow he'd received—managed to kick out at Brackett, knocking him against the rail.

Then they were struggling against the rail, with Mando choking Brackett with one hand, using the elbow of his bloody arm to push him back to where a two-stories drop waited.

"What . . . what're you doin', Peterson," Brackett gasped as Mando pressed down on him, "taking notes?"

I wasn't taking notes.

I was picking up the .44 Magnum, which weighed a ton. I was glad it did, because when I slammed the butt of it between his shoulder blades, Mando yowled with pain and let loose of Brackett, who slipped away from him, gulping at the air.

Mando made one last lunge at Brackett, and I do mean last, because the *Chronicle*'s star reporter stepped to one side, and the cadaverous SOB slammed into the railing, lost his balance, and did an Olympic dive onto the floor below, bouncing off a lab table along the way.

Now he was spread-eagled down there, his face staring up with empty eyes. It really was the face of a cadaver now.

But we didn't hang around to contemplate such ironies. We were scrambling up another flight of metal stairs to the top cell-block tier. Brackett was about to turn right when I tugged him left.

"Why that way?" he asked.

"I know where I'm going," I said.

"How?"

"I *work* here!"

He blinked. "Oh, yeah."

I opened the door, and we were on the landing of a stairwell. The sound of footsteps on the stairs below, and Willy Chess's voice, echoed up after us.

Moving quickly, I followed Brackett up. Way up. The doors to each floor were labeled, and when we were passing the eighth floor landing, I asked, "Where are we going?"

"All the way." He glanced back, and noticed I

was still lugging the late Mando's big revolver. "You want me to take that?" he said, breathing hard.

"Do you know how to use it?" I asked, breathing pretty hard myself as we scrambled up.

"Not . . . not really."

"I do."

The ninth floor.

"*You* know how to shoot a .44 Magnum?" he asked.

"Is that what this is?"

"I guess that answers my question."

"No it doesn't, smartass. Did a column called 'Self-defense and the '90s Woman.' Spent a lot of afternoons at the firing range."

Tenth floor.

"I feel so reassured," he said, panting.

I didn't say anything. Actually, I was getting a little winded, with all these damn stairs.

And now we were at the top, on a landing where a mop in a pail by a cleaning cart were against the wall near a stainless-steel door whose sign read AUTHORIZED PERSONNEL ONLY.

"That's you, kid," he said.

I inserted my security pass into the panel, and he grabbed the mop, and we stepped through.

We were on a small platform, high above the glowing glass dome of the research farm. Around us rose huge tanks and motors and ventilation shafts. Behind me, Brackett closed the door and made sure it would stay that way, jamming the mop handle through the panic bar.

"Not many options," he said, looking around.

Just one, really: A narrow metal grid, hung with rows of lighting fixtures that bathed the dome below, stretched across to another platform, and another door. The grid was partly a catwalk that allowed one person to go out and change lights. It wasn't really designed for two people.

"You first," he said.

"And here I thought chivalry was dead," I said.

I stepped onto the catwalk, holding on to the rail with one hand, the gun in my other. It was a wobbly structure, but serviceable.

"Come on," I called. "It'll hold us!"

I heard him step on, and felt the thing sway, and we started quickly across.

But before we got there, the door we were headed for opened—and there he was: Sam Smotherman, a.k.a. Ernesto Vargas.

"You killed Mando," he said. "You leave me no choice. I'll just have to do this myself."

He moved from the platform out onto the catwalk, holding on to the rail with one hand, leveling a revolver at us with the other.

I raised the .44 Magnum. It was big and heavy for me to shoot with one hand, but I needed the other to hang on, and my three shots—*bam! bam! bam!*—were wild, zinging off metal.

Smotherman jumped back a step. The catwalk swayed.

Behind me, Brackett sounded both flabbergasted and respectful. "You're full of surprises, Peterson," he said.

"Stay put," I told Smotherman tightly, "or I'll blow you away."

His smile was mocking. "I don't think so."

I fired. The kick of the damn thing! My bullet hit a light fixutre, sending sparks flying. The fixture broke loose and crashed through the glass dome and landed with a *krunk!* on the research farm floor, fifty feet below.

Smotherman may have been surprised by my nerve, but he had nerve of his own. He kept advancing, the revolver steady in one hand, his eyes glittering in the night.

So I fired again.

And this time I got him. In the leg, but I got him! It tore a gouge in his pantleg, exposing skin, cutting a gash, and he nearly toppled off the catwalk. His cry seemed more of anger than pain, though, and he held the gun out in a trembling arm, and dragged himself along the railing of the gridwork.

Why Smotherman kept coming, in the face of a .44 Magnum, I can't say. He knew I would shoot, and that I was even capable of hitting him. But he was determined, his expression wild, as if he were dizzy from the pain of the gaping wound I'd inflicted.

I was backing up, and so was Brackett, and I held the .44 as tightly and firmly in the insufficient one-handed grip as I possibly could, when the world damn near went out from under me.

My left heel had caught in one of the gridwork holes of the catwalk, and my balance went. My purse hooked on the metal railing, and for a moment I went backward, the big gun tumbling out of my hand, falling down into nowhere. My purse snapped open, its contents spilling out.

And among the many things that bounced onto that metal grating was the silver ballpoint pen I'd taken from Danny Brown's movie-house crash pad.

The pen hit the floor of the catwalk and rolled toward Smotherman and popped open.

And from inside, where it had been wrapped

around the cartridge, unspooled a small roll of microfiche.

I stared at it, incredulous.

"Well, what do you know," Smotherman said.

I moved forward, crouching, ready to reach for
the microfiche.

The click of Smotherman cocking the revolver
echoed ominously.

"Pete, old buddy," Smotherman called. He almost
sounded drunk. "Pay attention! I'm about to make
you a widower."

Steadying himself, the erstwhile Ernesto Vargas
pointed his gun right at me.

I had to assume Brackett saw it, too, but I
couldn't see him. All I could see was Smotherman
aiming the gun at my head.

Then I heard Brackett whisper: "Hold on tight."

I glanced behind me, and saw that Brackett had
backed up to where he could grasp a lever, which his
hand was poised to pull.

Suddenly, as if a trapdoor had been opened under
the world, the opposite half of the catwalk dropped
straight down like a falling beam, crashing through
and shattering the glass dome. As Brackett and I
clutched the rail, a stunned Smotherman lost his
balance, falling backward, his eyes wide with horror
as the catwalk turned into a gigantic, treacherous
slide that sent him careening down the length of the
grid. Brackett reached for him, but it was too late.

Smotherman didn't even have time to scream. He
just plunged off the edge and down to a waiting pit
of shattered glass.

We were hanging on for dear life, dangling inside
the dangling catwalk. I watched in frustration as the

roll of microfiche fluttered, caught in the grating, out of reach above us.

Then the microfiche roll, jarred by the sway of the catwalk, came loose and rolled down toward us. I let go of the rail so I could reach and grab for the tumbling roll, and found myself sliding, like Smotherman had, down the catwalk.

"Sabrina!"

He couldn't reach me.

But I could reach that microfiche, *and* reach out for the rail, catching it and myself.

I held up the microfiche of the LDF test results, like a prize, and said, "Yes!"

Below us, in the research farm, a dejected Willy Chess was standing, looking at the corpse of his college friend. Sirens were cutting the air. Willy didn't even seem to considering making a break for it.

But Willy would have more than just the law to answer to: He would have to face the father whose megabucks business he had squandered and shamed.

And the man who had been both Ernesto Vargas and Sam Smotherman—spawled facedown on a pile of broken glass, deader than his dreams—would not be rising from the ashes this time.

Brackett reached down toward me. "Now that this is over, maybe we should discuss our future."

I took his hand. "In case we don't have one, why not discuss it now?"

He pulled me up to him. "You *have* heard of community property, haven't you?"

He had an arm around my waist, but he was eyeing the microfiche.

"That's only for consummated marriages," I said.

"That's where the future comes in." His smile was, as usual, smug. "Maybe we should finish what we started."

26

A Final Word

BYLINE: Peter Brackett

Of course, we decided to stay married, though modern woman that she is, Peterson has remained Peterson (Peterson-Brackett is a byline that the thought of which makes us both a little ill) and our stories were (and continue to be) filed separately. Both of us were overlooked by the Pulitzer people, despite the national importance of the LDF cover-up.

But Hollywood and the world of publishing smiled on us, and this book represents our first official collaboration, although we're hoping, before long, to announce another collaboration. It's a project we've been working on rigorously.

We spent our first night back in Chicago not at

either of our apartments, but at a plush suite at the Drake. The morning after, we spent in bed reading the *Chronicle* and the *Globe* over a room-service champagne breakfast.

I read the *Globe*. She read the *Chronicle*. I read passages aloud from her article, she from mine. We both complimented each other on the sheer poetry of our words and the diligence of our reporting. We were on our honeymoon, after all.

"Maybe we should write that mystery novel, for Willy," I suggested.

She nestled next to me in bed. The shiner I'd given her was magnificent to behold. "Maybe we should—it'll give him something to read, inside. But you're the novelist."

"We could collaborate. How's this for an idea? The two top reporters in town—one a man, the other all woman—compete over a hot story. Along the way, they fall in and out of love, squabble, make up, narrowly survive encounters with various and sundry fiendish assassins, get naked in front of Boy Scouts— just the woman—do battle with bad guys in a mad scientist's lab, hang off a catwalk, make the world a safe place again for milk-drinking kids everywhere, then go on a honeymoon that lasts forever."

"Sounds like a bestseller to me."

Little Dick, the puppy I gave her, was curled up at the foot of the bed. He was snoring peacefully, having eaten most of both our breakfasts. We'd fed him lavishly to keep him from barking and alerting the management that we'd smuggled him in.

Sabrina had kept the dog boarded for such a long time, she couldn't bear to keep him "in jail" another day—not after seeing "those poor animals" at Chess Chemical.

"Peter," she was saying. "Did you really mean it?"

"What?"

"What you said last night?"

"I meant it all."

"Including that our double-crossing days are behind us?"

"Sure . . . but it can't be a one-way street."

She gave me a Scout's honor sign. "I'll go straight if you promise you will."

"I do," I said.

"I do, too," she said.

But in all honesty, I have to tell you I had my fingers crossed. And I noticed that Sabrina's legs were crossed at the time.

She snuggled against me and things were starting to get friendly when a siren came blaring down the street ouside the hotel. Sirens aren't unusual in Chicago, of course, but we could both tell the siren belonged to a vehicle that had stopped just ouside.

Sabrina hopped out of bed and went to the window and threw it open.

"Brackett!" she said. She grabbed a hotel note pad and pen off the writing table. "Two cops are getting out of a squad car, and they have their .38s out!"

I shook my head, went to the window, and turned her around. Took her pad and pen away.

"No." I said. "It's our honeymoon."

She gave me a crinkly smile, "I forgot for a second."

I kissed her. A nice, long, sweet kiss.

She nuzzled my neck. "I remember, now."

From this angle, I could see the cops heading across the street. Embracing her with one arm, I made a few notes on the pad, behind her back. But then Sabrina's hand flipped the pad away from us both, out the open window.

She kissed me, but I could tell she was peeking out there, so I shut the curtains and pulled her over to the bed.

Before resuming work on our collaboration in progress, I did take time out to push a chest of drawers in front of the door, blocking the old-fashioned keyhole.

After all, we're celebrities in this town, and you never know when some damn reporter might be snooping around.